## THE PRIDE OF THE DOUBLE DEUCE BOOK 3

# KATHI S. BARTON

This is a work of fiction. Names, characters, places, and incidents are products of the author's imagination or are used fictitiously and are not to be construed as real. Any resemblance to actual events, locations, organizations, or persons, living or dead, is entirely coincidental.

**World Castle Publishing, LLC**
Pensacola, Florida

Copyright © Kathi S. Barton 2015
Hardback ISBN: 9781629893617
Paperback ISBN: 9781629893624
eBook ISBN: 9781629893631
First Edition World Castle Publishing, LLC, November 30, 2015
http://www.worldcastlepublishing.com

**Licensing Notes**

Cover: Karen Fuller
Editor: Eric Johnston
Editor: Maxine Bringenberg

# CHAPTER 1

"I don't understand this." Susie looked at the paperwork in front of him, then at the man who was questioning her application. "It says here that you've spent some time in jail and that you've been...what does this word mean? Exonated?"

"Exonerated. It means that the charge of murder had been wrong and I was let out because they figured out that I didn't do it. I should never have been in jail at all, and that's what they're saying now." He nodded but still looked confused. "The next paper is a copy of my release. It tells you right there that I was—"

"Yeah, you said that." He stacked the papers up, including her application, and then handed them to her. "I don't think this will work out with us. We have customers coming in all the time and they don't want to be waited on by an ex-con. You'll have to go someplace else. Just don't expect anyone else to be as nice about you and your paperwork as I was."

Standing up, Susie wanted to scream at him that she wasn't an ex-con but a real person, and more than that, she'd not done a damned thing but be in the wrong place at the wrong time. Instead, she picked up her bag and coat and moved out of the office. *Now what*, her mind screamed at her. She had to find something soon or things were going to get really bad for her.

This was the ninth job that she'd applied for in the last three days. Her money, what she'd gotten as a compensation for being wrongly accused, was going out faster than she had anything coming in…which was not a single dollar. Even living as cheaply as she was, she'd be broke in another month. Less if she had to move out of the hotel she was staying in, because they had a two-week limit on how long someone could stay there. Every place else was double what she was paying now. Nothing, it seemed, was going her way.

Making her way back to the hotel, she bypassed the front office and just unlocked her door and entered. She didn't owe any money for the room just yet, but the guy at the counter this time of day made her feel dirty, like she'd been bathing in slime for an hour. Putting her things on the bed after locking the door, she sat in the chair and closed her eyes.

Five years she'd been in prison. Not a long time by some standards, and less than she had been sentenced to by a long shot. Her life sentence had been overturned, and she'd been let out a month after someone on the outside had admitted to the murder of the three people in a house she'd never been in, as well as a few others things the man had, up until then, gotten away with. He'd apparently had details that were never made public, and when he'd admitted to it, saying how proud he was to not get caught, she'd been told there had been a mistake.

"A fucking big one if you ask me." Susie Benjamin had never done a thing wrong in her entire life that would have gotten her into trouble. And certainly nothing like what she'd been accused of. She'd always been careful of what she did, what she said, and even what she'd written down. Having parents that were less than stellar had made her into a very cautious woman and extremely terrified of the cops. She supposed she might have been a little too cautious at times, but there was little she could do about it now.

Her mother had been in and out of jail most of Susie's young life. Then when Susie had turned ten, her mom, along with three other people, had robbed a convenience store and had killed the young man behind the counter as well as a few other customers. It had been planned, they said, and since they'd brought guns with them that were loaded with extra casings, it was considered premeditated. She'd been found guilty and sentenced to twenty-five to life in prison. Which, when it came down to it, had been a life sentence, because she'd died there. And because Susie had been a minor, the courts had called in her father to care for her.

It had been like going from the pan to the oven for her. Ernest Benjamin, Ernie to those few who were stupid enough to call him a friend, had been no better in caring for her than her mother, and he'd been meaner about it. The third time he'd hit her with his belt, she left. It had only taken them a week to find her and bring her back to his loving arms and his leather belt. And it never got any better after that. In fact, she'd say it was a good deal worse.

Over the next five years, Susie would run away monthly. Sometimes she'd be gone for a couple of weeks, but mostly she'd be found and taken back for a more severe beating, as well as being locked in her room without food or water. Not that it caused her many problems. Getting out was easy since she was small and strong, but he'd hurt her enough on her sixteenth birthday that someone finally took notice of her situation. He'd broken her arm, beaten her so badly that she'd had hundreds of stitches as well as the concussion that made her sick when she blinked.

But being put into foster care wasn't that much of an improvement. The home she'd been sent to first had been all right. She had to help around the house a lot, but that didn't bother her much. Then one day the man of the house had been hurt at work, and the wife had no more use for watching kids that would never be hers. She was dumped—no other word for what had happened after that—back into the system and into many homes with mean bastards or drug users for foster parents.

Then there was the freaky little thing that she could do that made her a target for bullies. Being a cougar was hard to hide when she got pissed. She had learned to control her, but it wasn't done overnight. That, unfortunately, wasn't all that she could do, but no one had found out about that. But her father knew, and that was bad enough.

Her ability to read animals and some people had gotten her into some major issues with her father. For some reason, he was under the impression he owned her, which, she supposed, he did as the leader of their leap, and she thought that he should simply go fuck himself and die. Her plan didn't work out so well.

The foster care, or the lack of it, lasted just until she was eighteen and able to move out on her own. And in that time she'd gotten her education—something that she wanted more than anything—and a job. It wasn't a good job, and the people she rented the house with took most of her checks, but the tips were all hers. Sometimes they amounted to more than her checks. Then when she'd turned nineteen, they came to her hovel and arrested her for murder.

The knock at the door, firm but not loud, startled her from her morbid thoughts. "Susan, there's a call for you." Susie didn't move from her position on the chair, but did glance over at the phone that had not rung since she'd been there. It was the only number she'd given out when she applied for jobs. Really, it was the only one she knew. "It's about the job at that bar down on Seventy-Nine."

Susie still didn't move. She'd not been anywhere near the state route, nor had she applied at a bar. She didn't drink and certainly didn't want to have anything to do with serving up drinks for men who got mean when they were drunk. When the guy at the door pounded on the door again, she moved to the bed to pick up the first thing she'd bought when she'd gotten out. The bat was her only defense now, and she wasn't afraid to use it.

The pounding got harder then, and she was sure the door was going to break under his fists. "Open the fucking door, Susan. I know that you're in there. I saw you go in." The voice sounded familiar, but she didn't know who it might be, as fear was making her too nervous to think beyond what he'd do when he got inside. As the pounding on the door got harder and louder, she moved to the back of the room and away from the room's only window, and near the bathroom door should she need to escape there. "You fucking cunt, open this goddamned door and let me in. I know that you have some cash, and I want it."

Then just like that, she knew who it was. Her father, Ernie. Still not going to the door, she reached for the phone just as he moved to the window and started beating it to shit. The service at the front desk answered right away. The window wasn't going to stand up to his abuse any better than the door had.

"You need to let him in so I don't have to call the cops. I don't need nothing like this going on here. This is a good family hotel and we don't cotton to having domestic fights between families. Get him to shut up." *Nice,* was all Susie could think about. And calling the cops would be less than preferable than her being beat to shit? No thanks.

"Call them. He's not coming in here. At least not unless he breaks down your door to do so. Or...fuck." The window burst inward, and he tore the curtains down just as she was putting the bat on her shoulder to use. "Come in here and they'll be taking you away in a body bag, you motherfucker."

"That's no way to talk to me, bitch. I'm your boss and you'll fucking do as I say, or so help me, Susan, you're gonna regret me having to make you." She wanted to laugh at him but didn't. Prison hadn't been good to him either, apparently. He was bruised on his face, nothing that had improved his looks, and his mouth had sores on it, like he'd had a blister and he'd worried it to death. When he started into the room again, screaming at her about what he wanted, she pointed the bat at him and made him pause. "I want what's coming to me. And I know you got it. That there paper said you were given completion or some shit like that. Ten grand will go a long way to making me a happy daddy."

"I'm not giving you shit. And it's compensation, you dumbass, not completion." He grinned at her, and she felt her skin crawl. His mouth was full of rotted teeth. And if that wasn't bad enough, his lips were dry and peeling and there were sores, big ones, on his cheeks and forehead she could see now that he was closer to her. "What the fuck is wrong with you now?"

"Nothing. But there will be with you when I get in there. You've been a disappointment to me since I squirted you in your mother. Where is she anyways?" He put his foot out to step into the room and then was gone. Not in that he fell back, or even into the room, but simply gone. Not trusting him or what he might be up to, she stood there with the bat ready in the event he returned. Then a woman was standing there messing with her hair. Her smile reminded Susie of the grandmother in those dumb card commercials. Like she was as happy as a lark.

"You all right?" Nodding slowly, she watched the woman carefully. There wasn't anything about her that was threatening, but Susie knew better than to trust anyone that she'd not touched at least once. "I won't hurt you. I was going by and saw him trying to get in, and couldn't let that happen. My name is Georgie Douglas."

"Yeah, and why should you care if he got in here or not?" The woman only nodded and moved away from the broken window. Then she knocked on the door. "You come in here without being invited and I'm going to knock you into next month. I don't need your help."

Going back to the broken window, the woman turned to her right before looking back at her. There was something very calming about the woman, as if she was just as nice as she looked. But again, Susie wasn't trusting her and stood her ground.

"My nephew's wife said that she's on her way. Normally she doesn't go out on calls because the mayor doesn't do that sort of thing, I guess, but she was riding with one of the cops that have been called. Your landlord called in that you were making a disturbance." Great, the mayor was coming, but Susie only watched her. "You're not very trusting, are you?"

"No shit." The woman looked pained for a second but said nothing. "What did you do to Ernie? And you should really watch out in case he comes back. Because he will now that he knows where I am. And if you hurt him, which I applaud by the way, you will be in as deep as shit as I am."

"He's going to be arrested. But he won't be coming back here. Come out of there and let me see if he hurt you, please. I feel just horrible that he was able to break this window before I could come to your rescue. Not that you need it. Which reminds me, why didn't you just take care of him yourself? You could have." Susie wanted to move…felt like it was the only thing in the world she wanted to do, but she shook her head and felt better. "You're very strong, aren't you? I mean…well, you shouldn't have been able to toss off my compulsion like that. You're a cougar, aren't you?"

"So?" She felt her cat move along her skin but didn't let her out. She had a great deal of control over her now, not like the little she'd had when she was younger. "So are you. But that doesn't mean that we're going to be the best of friends."

Georgie only smiled at her, and that was when Susie heard the sirens. Her body tensed up to the point where she wanted to run. It was as ingrained in her as much as breathing. Cops meant trouble, and trouble meant jail. Not necessarily, but it seemed that way to her and her cat.

When the cops came to the door, it exploded open with no more than someone pushing against it hard. A man entered, his gun drawn and his face hard, and she knew that he, too, was a shifter, but not a cat. Wolf. When he pointed the gun at her and told her to drop her weapon, she did so without having to be asked twice.

The woman who came in behind him told him to back down. "Did you hear a word I told you on the way here? That the woman in the room was not to be...put that fucking gun down before I hit you."

The gun was lowered, but he didn't put it in his holster. Instead, he turned and looked at the woman with a sneer on his face. "You should know that I don't take direct orders from you."

The woman nodded and then did the most amazing thing. She punched the man in the face, and he fell to his knees. As he was getting up, to no doubt hit the woman, she spoke, her words as soft as a gentle rain.

"You do and you'll be dead before you take your next piss." He paused, fear only a little evident on his face. "You know who I am, and let me tell you that I've already contacted your alpha and told him what you've done."

"He's on his way out too. I'm telling you that you're just a little speck on my way to the top of the heap." She asked him if he really believed that. "I do. He's done nothing but coddle the pack for years now, and it is time for someone with a backbone to bring it around. He's happier to hang around with you cats than he is to see to our needs. He has to go, and I'm going to be the one to take him out."

"I'll be sure to tell him your opinion." Two more cops came into the room with them, and the woman turned to them after taking a step back from the cop on the floor. "I want him arrested. I'll give you the charges in—"

The wolf lunged at the woman, and before Susie could think what a horribly terrible idea it was, she let her cat take her and leapt at the cop. He was dead before she finished shifting, her claws raking across his throat even as she took him to the floor. His head rolled toward the woman as Susie's cat backed them into a corner. She was in deep shit, she just knew it.

~~~

Mason entered the station as calmly as he could. When Aunt Georgie had reached out to him a little while ago, she'd told him to come to the station but not to make a big deal out of things. He'd felt Emma's anger and then her fear, then nothing. It wasn't until Aunt Georgie had told him that she'd bumped her head but was all right now that he could reach out to his wife. Emma had some explaining to do.

*Don't make me have to explain why my big bad husband had to come in here and make it all better. If you do, everything I've worked for will be for nothing.* He asked her calmly, or as calmly as he could, what had happened. *I was stupid. I turned my back on someone when I knew better. But I'm fine.*

*That does not leave me with a warm and fuzzy feeling, Emma. I felt your terror and it nearly took me to my knees. Please, I beg of you. What happened?* She told him she'd explain it to him when he got there, but not to make a scene.

The first person he saw when he came into the front of the station house was his aunt. Her smiling at him had him thinking that someone needed to be punched. Not her, of course, but someone, and soon. She was entirely too mean to hit and not expect to be hit back.

"She's fine. Shook up a bit but fine. She's back there talking to the woman who saved her butt. That man...oh my Mason, he was going to kill our little Emma, and if that...if that other woman had not changed and took him, I'm not sure how it would have ended."

This wasn't helping him or his cat. Mason had been out on the range with ten men when he'd nearly cut his hand off because the knife he'd been using slipped. They'd been putting up a fence that had been knocked over by a fallen tree and he'd been in charge of cutting the old wire off. Had Gerard or Jace not been there, he wasn't sure what he'd have done.

"Can I see her now?" Aunt Georgie told him she was calming the other cat...the one that had saved her. "What other cat? You mean another cougar is here?"

"Two actually. Her father and this young woman. I saved her first, so you know. I'm telling you that so you don't find out later and get upset with me. I was there visiting a friend of mine who has only just moved to this area, and I heard the commotion. She and her family have been wanting to move to this area for some time, and they've put a bid on a house close to the ranches. But there was this man, as I was saying. He was going to go and hurt the girl. I just had to act. Good thing too. I think he was going to kill her."

Mason only stared at his aunt. He was getting more and more confused by the second. Two cougars were here? And who was the woman and man? He started to ask her what the hell she was talking about when she smiled at him.

"You're confused. I'm sorry. To be honest with you, I'm a little shook up myself. But let me explain. There was this man who was trying to hurt who I found out later was his daughter. She wasn't having him in her room, so he busted out the front window. Then he—"

"Aunt Georgie." She smiled at him. "I love you very much, but you're driving me insane with this roundabout story. Either get to some point so my cat will be happy or…you know what? Never mind. Am I going to get to see Emma any time soon?"

Then Mason felt her. She was coming through the door just as his aunt started again about her friend. As he moved around his aunt to see his wife, Emma nearly fell into his arms. Mason held her for several minutes before she lifted her chin up to look at him. There was a small stain of blood on her cheek, but he knew that it wasn't hers. Mason asked her if she was all right.

"Yes, I am, thanks to the…I want you to know that this girl is the most stubborn woman I have…I thought you said that I could make people talk to me when they didn't want to. And especially other cougars." He said that was true. "Well, not with this woman. She's as tight lipped as I've ever seen anyone be. And she just shakes off the compulsion like it's nothing. I think she's a half breed…is that what you call people who aren't all cat? But I really don't know. She could be a mountain goat for all I can get from her."

"I'm sure you'd know if she was a goat or not. Now, who is she?" Emma said she was still trying to work that out, but she did ask him to talk to her. "Talk to her about what? I'm assuming that you've arrested her or had her arrested?"

"No. She did nothing wrong as far as I'm concerned. She's free to go, but she just sits there staring at her lap like it's got all the answers. The most I've gotten out of her is that the man that Aunt George knocked out is her father, and that didn't come from her but from him. And let me tell you, he's not shut up since he woke up. I have never met two people that are more ill-suited to be related in my life. She just calmly sits there while he spouts off about suing us and having your aunt arrested for poor treatment of him.

Bastard. But I can feel her fear, Mason. She's terrified of something or someone." He asked her if she thought it was her. "I didn't do anything to her. And if that were the case, why save me?"

"I'll talk to her, but I don't know if I'll have any more luck than you did. If she throws off the compulsion, she might belong to another alpha. Or has pledged to one. Whatever the reason, she should have let us know she was here and how long she was staying. It's the law of our kind and she should have known that." He was shown to the room she was in and turned to Emma when she started to go in with him. "This might be better if you let me handle her. I'm not sure what might happen, and if she shifts again she's going to pull both our cats, and that won't be good."

"Don't hurt her." Mason turned to look at her before he opened the door. "Just…trust me on this when I tell you that she'll drive you to want to hurt her, but don't. There is something profoundly sad about her that I don't think she's handling as well as she'd like to think she is."

"Even though you don't know her, you can feel this from her." Emma nodded. "Are you thinking that this man, her father, should be brought in as well? I mean for me to talk to?"

"Oh yeah, that's a given. But for now, I think you should just go easy on her. And you should know that your aunt is looking into some things. She said that she could smell Calendar on her, the guy at the restaurant that you had words with the other night. I think she might have had a run-in with him too." He grinned. The man had been making passes at his staff and then taking away some of their checks for no good reason other than they'd not have sex with him. Mason had fun showing him the error of his ways. Zach had even helped him. "This is no time to tell me

17

how proud you are of yourself. You could have hurt that man."

"But I didn't, and I'm pretty sure that when he finds out who my aunt is related to, he's going to be falling all over himself to help her." Emma only sighed heavily. "What is it, Emma? This girl, what is it that has you so worked up?"

"I have no idea. For all I know she could be this terrible person who runs over small dogs in her free time. But there is something about her that makes me want to protect her." He moved away from the door and took her into his arms. "Just don't let her get hurt, Mason. By you or anyone else. For all her stubbornness, I think I like her. And she saved me from having to explain to you why I got hurt."

Kissing her again, he went to the door and let out a long breath. He was sort of nervous if he was honest with himself, but he opened the door and moved into the room.

A man was standing behind her, another cop...a wolf that he knew from the local pack. She didn't look up when he came into the room, but he could see by the stiffness of her body that she knew just who he was. Either that or she was bracing herself for pain. Either way, he had to take charge right now.

"Do you know what I am?" She nodded but didn't lift her head. "Look at me when I talk to you."

As her head lifted, he could see the blood on her face. He didn't see a cut, but there was enough blood there to tell him she'd been hurt. Walking to her, he lifted her chin up and saw that her nose had been bleeding recently, and wondered if it was from when Emma had been in here. Fighting compulsions, especially from a leader, was hard on a person. Telling the cop to go and get her a wash cloth, Mason sat down in front of her.

"Tell me who you are." He could see her fighting him. Christ, she was strong, and when she shivered he knew that she'd won this round. "Tell me who you are now. And what that man at the hotel wanted from you."

She lost, but at great cost to herself. The blood at her nose from the pain of what she was doing wasn't all that happened to her. When she looked at him, he could see the anger too. She'd also bitten her lip through, and the swelling was making his heart pull.

"Susan Benjamin." He didn't think she was going to answer all of his questions, but she put her hands on the table and glared at him. Instead of pissing him off, Mason found himself liking her. "I'm not an ex-con, and that man, my father, will kill me as soon as I'm set free. If he doesn't do the deed himself, I will do it for him because I'm not going to do what he wants."

Reaching for Emma, he let her know what she'd said about not being an ex-con and asked her to look into it. He looked at the girl. "What are you doing in this town without telling me who you are and why you are here?" He could see the confusion on her face, so he explained. "I'm the leader of this leap, and by law you have to report to me, or whoever is in charge, of your presence."

"Why?" He really didn't know for sure why, but he knew it was law. "Not that it matters. I'm going to move on as soon as I'm sure that Ernie is going to be under lock and key for a while."

"Ernie would be your father?" She nodded and wiped the blood off her upper lip. "You'd not hurt if you'd just answer the questions instead of being stubborn. You know that, don't you?"

"Fuck off." He nearly laughed at her but only just caught himself. "Am I in trouble? Can I leave? Or are you going to keep me here under some trumped-up charges for killing that fuck?"

"The other cop?" She didn't even blink in his direction. "I have no control of what happens to you about the wolf you killed. His alpha is coming in here to talk to you as well. If he has any kind of punishment in mind, I can take care of that for—"

"No. You stay out of it. That would be between the two of us, nothing to do with you." He nodded, but knew as surely as he was sitting there with her that he'd intercede on her part. "What happens to Ernie?"

"I don't know. I'm not a cop, nor do I try and interfere with their laws." The snort coming from Susan had him covering his mouth. She really was about as stubborn a person as he'd ever met. "What were you doing there? I mean, why are you here?"

"Didn't she tell you yet?" He leaned back in his chair and asked her who. "Your wife. The mayor. I'm assuming that as soon as you told her that I'm not an ex-con and what my name is, she got right on that. But let me tell you now. I'm moving on as soon as I find out where Ernie is and how long he's going to be there."

"I'm afraid I can't let you do that." She glared harder. He had no idea why he'd said that she couldn't leave just yet, and was afraid she'd ask him. "You broke the law, and even if you weren't aware of it, you still did it. There will be repercussions for your actions, and as soon as you're free from here, you'll report to me."

Mason stood up, and so did she. She was tall, nearly as tall as him. And he had a feeling that her cat was going to be big as well. He was going to have to ask Emma. When she did nothing more than stare at him, Mason had a sudden thought. She was terrified.

"What will you have me do? Be tied to a post while you beat me? I won't take it again. Or do you plan to put me in a cell, lock me away for another five years? If that's your plan, then I'd prefer that you fight me and kill me." Mason was so shocked by her words that he did not do or say anything. "I won't be treated that way again. Do you hear me? I'm not going to live if you do that."

When she leapt at him, it was all he could do to keep her from hurting him. When he flipped her to her back and held her down with his weight, he thought for sure she was going to shift. He stopped her with a single command. And when she stilled, he watched her.

"You thought that if you attacked me, I'd kill you. Was that your grand plan? To have me kill you so that whatever kind of thoughts are going on in your head wouldn't happen?" She only stared up at him. "Answer me, damn it. I've had a shitty morning so far, and you're so not helping it."

Nothing. Not a single word passed her lips, and he could see what it was costing her. When he commanded her again, just to see how far he could push her, she passed out, and Mason felt that this was only the beginning of the feud between them. For some reason, he was looking forward to it.

Calling to the guard to have her taken to his home, he hoped to Christ he wasn't making the biggest mistake of his life. Or that of his family if she decided to take some of her anger out on them. But he had a feeling that once tamed, she was going to be a hell of an ally.

# CHAPTER 2

Gerard watched as the shelves were filled. Items too large for the shelves were simply placed in the middle of the mill. He'd agreed to oversee this part of the new operation that his family was getting into, and wanted to make sure that everything was just the way he wanted it. When Aunt Georgie and Palmer walked in, he went to greet them and show them around if they had time. But the closer he got to them, the more he could see that something was wrong. Even his cat was a little on the nervous side when he got to them.

"Everything is fine." He nodded but peered over his aunt's head to look at Palmer. He nodded that she was telling him the truth. "We just had a few things going on at the jail and I had Palmer come to get me. We were going to pick out some new carpet for the library anyway."

Palmer was in love with Gerard's aunt. Any fool could see that. She kept telling them all that he wasn't her mate, but Gerard wasn't so sure about that. He could see the look in his aunt's eye every time they were together, and how she looked when another female got too close to Palmer. If he wasn't her mate, they were making a good show of it being true anyway. There was no hope if these two couldn't be mates, not for any of them.

He asked about the jail. After he was told the story, he still didn't have any idea why his aunt was upset, even after she told them Emma was saved by another cat and left for the bathroom to "freshen up." As soon as she was gone, Palmer smiled at him.

"Nothing really is wrong. She's fine. I think what has her worried is that girl. The one that saved our Emma." Gerard asked if Mason was pissed off. "No. I think he thought it was funny too. This woman is so headstrong that I think she might even have my little Holly beat on her stubbornness. But neither he nor Emma seemed upset about that. I think they like her, despite all the hoopla. Now he's got her under house arrest, so to speak, and she'll be working for him for a time. Her father is the one that has me worried. You might have heard of him. Ernest Benjamin."

"No. Should I have?"

They both turned when Aunt Georgie could be heard behind them. She looked better. Her face was free of worry, and he smiled at the fact that she was fussing at one of the workers about their language. She would curse up a storm if she was mad enough, but that didn't happen often. So whatever the man had said that she was glaring at, it must have been bad. The guy was on his knees begging her to forgive him.

When that was finished, he talked them into going to the office in the back so he could find out what was going on. He was sure it was going to be more than he wanted to know about a stranger.

"Ernest Benjamin, Ernie to those that know him, is the worst kind of person. He and his wife—I can't remember her name right now—were into drugs, murder, and mayhem. You name it and they had a part in it, I'm sure. He'd been married three or four times in the past, but one thing or another led up to their death...until he married a woman that by all accounts was worse than him. Anna—that's her name—had a baby, and only because I know how the mating thing works, they were suited to each other in more ways than just their inability to stay on the good side of the law. But it turns out they had a wonderful child. Susan Benjamin." Gerard asked if it was the woman at the jail. "Yes. Their daughter. And the exact opposite of them in every way possible. But then something happened. I'm not entirely sure what led to her being arrested for the murder of three people a few years ago, but they broke down her apartment door and beat her up pretty badly before she got to jail. Knowing a little about your kind, like I said, had she resisted arrest as they said she did, she could very well have killed them, but she only let them beat on her until she was unconscious. That's another thing that has me thinking that this girl is more than a little stubborn. I would think you'd have to have great control over your cat should you be hurt, right?"

"Yes. A great deal. Are both her parents cougars?" Palmer said he didn't know because her mother was dead; a fight in prison had taken her life. "So, this Susan person was in prison but now out. Do you know why, and what this has to do with the trouble at the jail?"

"She was exonerated. All charges were dropped, and they gave her a nice little cash settlement in exchange for her not suing them. I'm not sure what went on there, but I'm having it looked into." Gerard almost felt sorry for whomever was going to be on the chopping block when Palmer found his man. He was ruthless and a little scary when he was pissed off. "Anyway, according to Mason, she wasn't aware that she had to answer to him while here, or to report to him. I'm thinking that because of Emma liking her and all, he's making up this thing about her having to pay back some sort of fine for not reporting to him."

"No. He can do it." Palmer nodded, but Gerard explained. "She should have known about reporting to him, and even if she didn't, fighting him and Emma should have gotten her into hot water. There could have been some pretty hefty fines that went along with it too, but I guess he's not going that route. But what I don't understand is why they care."

Neither Georgie nor Palmer did either. When the next truck came to the loading dock to be unloaded, he left them with the promise that he'd be home for dinner tomorrow. He had to be on the ranch tomorrow anyway. That was why he was working so hard to get this place set up today. It was going to be a long day at the Double Deuce for all of them.

~~~

They'd gone together and bought the Mitchell ranch, as was the plan. No easy feat, since the man refused to take what they were offering. So when the bank came in, he'd lost it all anyway. When foreclosure was on him and his family, he had barricaded himself in the house with his family with a shotgun and refused to move out. It had ended badly; Mitchell and his oldest son had been killed. The wife and her two daughters had moved away just last week. They seemed to be thrilled to be free of the ranch and the man who had owned it. Once it was settled that they'd had no part in the police being called in, they left so quickly that they'd left everything behind. The house needed to be cleared out, as well as all the barns and out buildings.

"How many cows you got yourself now? I think they're all pretty and stuff when they just stand around in the grass. You think they don't mind the rain none?" He nearly snarled at the man when he spoke behind him, startling him and his cat. He didn't look familiar, so Gerard didn't answer him. When he smiled, it was like looking at a big boy in a man's body. He looked sort of...off, and not very friendly. "You not going to tell me?"

"I don't know you at all, so telling you private information isn't going to happen." The man grinned again. "How did you get in here? We're not open for business just now."

"I got my ways. I know this place pretty good. It's part of my family history. You know?" He turned and looked around the stockroom before looking at him again. "Yeah, this place looks real good. It would be a real shame should it go up in flames, don't you think? I like fire."

As the man lit his cigarette and then blew the smoke in Gerard's direction, Gerard reached for the men in the building with him. There were only two others, but they were wolf and would come to his aide now. As they told him they were coming, Gerard told Mason what was going on. Then Jace joined in the conversation.

*Do you know anything about him?* He told his brothers that he didn't know him at all. *But he's threatening you? Right there, just telling you that he's going to burn the place down?*

Gerard had to smile. Jace still had no idea how ruthless men could be sometimes. Well, maybe he did, but it was funny when he was reminded of it again and again. Mason had a better handle on that sort of thing, but Jace liked everyone and everyone seemed to like him. Gerard told him that he wasn't coming out and saying it, but close enough.

*We're coming. Don't do anything stupid.* Gerard asked Mason to define stupid. *Don't kill him. We have enough shit going on right now without you being in jail when we need you here.*

*But maybe I want to be in jail instead of cleaning out a house that means little to me.* Mason laughed, and Gerard felt a little better. *Hurry. I have two men here with me, and I'd just as soon none of us got hurt.*

Gerard realized he might have missed something the man said when he just cocked a brow at him. "What are you doing here? And what the hell do you think you're doing threatening me?" The man only laughed and looked to Gerard's left, then right. He knew that the other two had shown up to stand there, but he was worried that one or all of them was going to get hurt. "I asked you a question, jackass. What are you doing here?"

"You and your family, they got no right to be taking over things that don't belong to you. My brother told me that. I mean, I've been sent by someone that wants to make an example of you all, and he doesn't care who is hurt when he does it. He said that I could help him." The cigarette was flipped at him, but Gerard didn't flinch. Instead he ground it out with the toe of his boot and looked at the man. "This place don't belong to you. You know that, right? You stole it from the people who owned it."

Gerard repeated what he'd said to his brothers. He knew they were getting closer, but the man moved around him to the other end of the dock and where the other two men were standing. He supposed he could have done something then, but he didn't want to hurt anyone if he didn't have to. When the man looked into the big truck and turned to him, Gerard felt his cat move along his skin.

"Come back here and I'll kill you." The man only laughed and spit on the floor between his feet. "You will regret that."

"Why would I regret spitting on the floor?" Gerard didn't say anything…he had a feeling the man was a little slow, but maybe it was an act. "Well, I guess you gotta do what you gotta do, as my dad used to say to me. He's dead, you know? I think that my brother did it, but I don't know for sure. He can be really mean when he…I should be quiet now. He don't like it none when I'm too talky."

He jumped off the loading dock and moved away. Gerard felt his cat again and calmed him with the knowledge that the human had left them a calling card. Leaning down to the dirt, he rubbed his fingers into the spit and took it to his nose. Then he offered it to the wolves with him, and they all took the scent into their noses. The man was as good as right beside them now.

"Called in the alpha. He was in town so he's coming by." Gerard nodded at Dave, the wolf that had come from the front of the store to help him out. Jamie, the other man with him, only grinned when he glanced at him. But Dave spoke again and it sent a chill down his back. "He said that he'll not get within ten feet of this building or any of the other ones so long as he has breath in his body."

"Can you ask him to send a few men out to the ranch houses too?" Dave said it was already done. "Good. I'll let my brothers know, but I think that we'll try and keep things close to home for a little while. I don't know what this guy thinks he's about, but I'm going to find out what I can about the guy who ran the mill before it went under. I don't think it was him, but he knows him, don't you think?" They both agreed there was something there, but neither of them could figure it out either.

Garth Vance had skipped town right after the banker, Nigel Rogers, had been caught. His story of being insane hadn't stuck with the judge any more than it had with any of them. And Clark, their lawyer, had been the first to figure it out. Vance had not been seen or heard from since the Feds had come in and taken over the buildings. It wasn't until recently that they'd said the mill and the bank could be reopened, but with restrictions, one of them being that the Feds had to approve the men that were running the places. Gerard had been asked to step in and help them out. He was glad for the work, as he didn't think ranching was really in his blood.

After his brothers showed up and were given the man's scent, the three of them began looking for ways that the man might have gotten in. They found the basement doors weren't the only places showing signs of a break-in, but the windows all along the main floor had been tampered with too. Mason called in a security team to get cameras and a better locking system, but Gerard wondered if they were shutting the barn door after the cows had been put out to pasture. He didn't want to think of what it would do to have this place go up in flames.

They worked until nearly one in the morning making sure the place was as safe as they could get it. He made it to the house just as the sun was coming up, and didn't stir when he smelled the bacon frying in the kitchen down the hall.

~~~

Susie knew that she had to get up from the bed, but she was hoping that if she didn't move she could pretend, at least for a little while, that everything that had happened in the last twenty-four hours had been a dream. A bad one but a dream all the same. But lying there, she knew, would solve nothing. Sitting up, she looked around the room she'd been shown to last night when she'd gotten up from the couch.

The room she was in was nice. Probably the nicest one she'd ever be able to stay in again. At least for the next month anyway. The people she was staying with, Mason and Emma Douglas, had ordered her to stay with them and said that she'd be working for the ranch until the end of her sentence. She was pretty sure they were making that part up, but since she had no idea if they were lying or not, she'd told them she'd do what they said. And Susie was honest, despite what others might say about her. Getting up and moving to the bathroom, she snatched up her bag and took it in with her. It was all she owned in the world right now.

The water was hot, but she didn't want to waste it so took a quick shower. The need to linger under the hot strong spray had her hurrying faster, and she was standing in the bathroom with a towel around her waist when she heard someone knock on the bedroom door. Not bothering to answer, she finished brushing her teeth and then came out to find a strange man in the room. He nodded to her as he put a tray on the little table by the window.

"Mistress Emma asked that you come to see her when you have finished up here. She is at the office until four this afternoon. I have taken the liberty of making you a large breakfast, but should you desire something different, please let me know. My name is Randy Byrd, butler of this home." Susie nodded at him as he stood there. "You are very beautiful, if you do not mind me saying so, my lady."

"I'm not going to have sex with you." The moment she said it she hated herself for it and told him she was sorry. "I don't have a lot of trust for people, men especially. And lately, the last five years or so, I've been in a place that lent more to the distrust of people than trusting them. I'm very sorry."

"That's fine. I mean, I'm…Mistress Emma has told me of your life. And I'm sorry for my words. I should have taken better care than to say them to a stranger. But you are quite lovely." He nodded at her again and left her to herself.

The idea not to eat what was on the plate was tempting. And she might have been able to resist had her mouth not been watering over the scents coming from the covered dishes since the man had come into the room. Walking to the tray, she told herself that she was only going to eat the toast, but knew as soon as she saw the eggs and bacon she was going to devour it all. It had been forever since she'd had a crappy meal, and longer than that since she'd had a good one. Susie finished off the entire meal in less time than it took to make her bed and clean up after herself.

Taking the tray to the kitchen, she was surprised to find Mason there with four other men. They were related, any fool could see that, but she still paused in the doorway until Randy, the butler, took the tray from her.

"Hello. Did you sleep well?" Susie wasn't sure how to answer the man. She didn't understand why he cared, but he only grinned at her. "My name is Jace Douglas. These two are my brothers, Zach and Logan. We're waiting on Gerard and Darin, two more brothers, to join us while we eat Mason out of house and home."

"Susie Benjamin." Mason stood up, and she took a step back from him. It wasn't that he'd hurt her, but she didn't want him to be close enough to try. "Where am I to work off my punishment?"

"Do you cook or clean?" She told him she could do both, but not well on the cooking part. "How about ranching? Do you know anything about cattle and milkers?"

"I worked in the prison barn." She'd run it, but didn't say that to him. It wasn't any of his business, but if she could work outside instead of in the house, she might even give him her life history. "If you don't mind, I'll muck stalls rather than be inside."

"I don't think you're gonna have to do that, but we do need to go and clean out a barn and several outbuildings. The barn has been...the steer are gone for the most part, but we have to clean things up for the new cattle coming in. There are some horses too. I don't know how many, but there are a few of them that are out and about. The barns need to be stripped and redone. That means the feed has to be taken out and burned. You up for that?" She nodded and watched him in the event that he slapped her around. He didn't strike her as the hitting type, but then people, all of them, had all kinds of hidden talents. "If you'd go on out with Logan and get a start on the feed barn, I'd be grateful. If it's too much, let him know and I'll find you something else."

As she followed the other man out, she felt the sun on her face and paused long enough to let it burn on her face for several seconds. The man she was with, Logan, only waited for her, not making fun of her or saying anything nasty to her. And when she moved to go again, he never questioned what she'd done, but she did see him smile.

"The ranch that we're working on has been left in poor shape by the previous owners. It's not that he didn't feed his herd, but he didn't give them fresh food even though he had a stockpile in the barn. We looked it over and figured out that rather than take a chance on any more of them falling ill, we'd start fresh. The horses that Mason was telling you about have been set free for some reason. There are as many as a dozen in the other paddock, but other than that, we don't know." She nodded as she got into the truck with him. "Mason said that you're to take it easy today. He doesn't want you hurt."

Saying nothing but thinking hard, she knew that she'd work harder than anyone else even if it killed her, just to prove the big cougar wrong on what she could and couldn't do. It was childish, she knew, but she didn't want to be there any more than he wanted her there. She wasn't a person to slack off, and if she was set to a job, then she'd, by God, give it her all. This one, even under the circumstances, wasn't going to be any different.

As soon as the truck came to a stop, she could only stare at the shape everything was in. The barns were missing parts of the roof. There was fencing down all around the big corral, and the two horses there looked to be as underfed as she'd been lately. Their bones were showing, and their coat was dull with unhealthiness. She felt her heart break for them.

"We can't get too close to them." She asked Logan why not. "They're not used to our kind. I'm not sure even that many humans can get close to them. But if they don't get help soon, we're going to have to put them down rather than see them suffer. There were five of them that stayed pretty close to the barn, but they've already passed away. The vet seemed to think these two will as well if they don't start to trust us."

Not been killed but passed away. She moved to the fence and Logan cautioned her twice before she gave a soft whistle as she climbed up on the railing. Their ears flickered but neither of them moved in her direction. Getting down and on the other side of the fence, she felt Logan come near but not touch the fencing. She asked him to stand back as she made her way to two of the prettiest horses she'd ever seen, despite their being sick.

The first horse, the smaller of the two, was skittish. He kept dancing away from her, and she kept an eye on him as she moved to the other horse. Susie had always been good with animals because of what she could do, and it mattered little to them if she was human or not. It was the one thing she loved about working in the barn, getting to touch and be with other animals like her.

"Come on, buddy. You know you want to come to me. I can touch you if you let me." His ears flickered in her direction, but he didn't move. "I've been hurt, too, by people. Most of them were animals, but not like us, huh?"

He moved away from her, and she stopped moving. He was turned in her direction now, and she stared at him as he moved his head up and down, as if he was agreeing with her. She put out her hand and spoke to him again.

"I don't have anything to give you. If I had an apple, I'd split it with you if you let me touch you. Do you like apples?" He didn't move when she took several steps toward him. "I love them. Not all kinds, just a few. There are these ones called Gala that you'd like, I think. They're a little on the tart side, but oh so good when you bite into a nice crisp one."

Susie was within inches of touching his nose. The other horse was still now, taking his cues, no doubt, from the older horse. When he put his head down and she ran her fingers down his soft nose, she took the last two steps toward him. His head touched her forehead as she curled her fingers into his mane. As soon as she touched him, she knew that he was hurting. Not just because he'd not been treated well, but because his mate was gone, along with his child.

Susie had never told anyone what she could do. Not even when she'd been in prison had she mentioned that she and animals had a deeper connection than most adults. While not able to talk to all the creatures she encountered, she could hear them. This one she could talk to. When she felt the other horse come up to her, she reached out her hand and let him touch her too.

Susie felt someone touch her mind just as she was running her hand down the flanks of the smaller horse. She only glanced at Mason, who was at the fence now.

*Are they going to be all right?* She told him that would depend on him, she supposed. *Fair enough. But what I meant was, do you think you can get him to let the vet look him over? And the other one?*

*They're both in good health. They need water, fresh water if you don't mind, and the larger horse needs to have his left rear foot looked at.* Susie moved to the other side of the horse and saw the long marks of a whip on his belly and flanks. *Someone has beaten them. Was it you?*

*No. I don't beat animals any more than I do people.* She only looked at him. *You're not at all trusting, are you? No, Susan, I didn't beat them. They were like they are when we got them out of the barn three days ago. Or I should say when they charged out of the barn three days ago. We've been leaving them fresh food, but I'm sorry to say I never thought of the water situation. I'll have it done now.*

*Susie, not Susan.* She moved to the barn where there were two men, and both horses followed her. *Do you happen to know where I can buy an apple or two? I promised him one should he let me touch him.*

*I have one in the truck, as a matter of fact. Will you come for it, or will I need to lay it out for you to give him?* She led the horse to the barn where Mason was, and he moved to get the apple. When he started to hand it over to her, she told him to give it to the horse. When the horse took it from Mason, she smiled at the animal. He was going to be all right now, she thought.

Going into the barn, she picked up a pitch fork and began emptying the feeders of all the meal that was in them. She could see the mold now, and the rats had been in it as well. Susie turned when Mason said her name.

"How did you do that?" She asked him what. "You know what. That horse had been slated to be put down because no one could get within ten feet of him, and Logan said you just walked out there and he came right to you."

There wasn't a question, so she didn't have an answer for him. She supposed he did ask her how she'd done it, but she didn't have an answer to that either, so she didn't say anything. But when he crossed his arms over his chest and asked her again, she turned her back to him and worked as she answered him. Now that she was a part of his leap, even temporarily, she had to answer him. It was that or risk having her sentence extended, as well as another whopping headache.

"I have a way with animals is all. They...I get along better with them than I do with people. Shifters or just regular people. It doesn't really matter, but we get along better. They're not as...abrasive to me." He asked her what that meant. She wondered if he meant the abrasive part or just getting along. Susie decided to answer it in a way that wouldn't get her into trouble again. "I don't know really.

They…we have a connection of sorts. I don't hurt them and they trust me. And I trust them as well."

"Can you talk to them? Can they talk to you?" She told him not always. "Then how do you know what they need? How they feel?"

"I don't know that either. I just…like I said, we have a connection. It's their…everything. Emotions. Hurt. Hunger. Sadness." She turned to look at him then, and his huge body was outlined in the barn door. There was something calming about his stance. She had no idea why, but she thought she could trust him if it came to something bad. "I won't bother them any more if you don't want me to. But I don't want to work inside. If you leave me outside, I won't do anything with the animals anymore."

"But you will if I need you to? You'll help me with them should I ask you to help me?" She was confused but nodded at him. "Good. That's good to know. I might. Need you, I mean. And soon. And if you want to work with them, go ahead. I'm sure that both of you, you and the horses, could use a friend about now. At least until you begin to trust us."

When he left, she started on the second stall. Logan came in to help her, and they worked through the morning on the stalls. By noon they had them all cleaned out and the feed, nasty shit, taken out to the large pile that was set to be burned in a few days. She was taking the last to the burn pile when she was introduced to Holly Douglas and the rest of the men of the family.

"Gerard isn't here, but he'll be here by dinner. There are some problems in town that he has to deal with." Susie said nothing as Logan told her this. "You'll like him, too."

Moving to the lunch tables that had been set up while she'd been working, she wondered why he thought she'd like any of them. They were just a job, and the sooner she was gone, the better she'd be. And the further away she could get from her father, the safer she'd be too. Or she would be until he found her again.

# CHAPTER 3

The house was quiet when he moved into the living room. Gerard had been so busy today that he was bone tired, and sore even. The thought of shifting and moving into the trees beyond the house was so tempting that he moved past the kitchen, where he knew a meal was waiting on him, to the deck surrounding the house. He was glad now that he'd been staying with Jace and Holly. They had the densest woods he'd ever been in. He was naked by the time he moved off the deck, and was just about to shift when he felt her. Turning slowly, he looked at the large cougar and put his hands up with a grin.

"Hi. You caught me at a disadvantage, I'm afraid." She snarled at him and moved back. "Don't run. If you do, I'm going to shift and chase you. I've had a really shitty day, and my cat would love to take it out on a trespasser right about now."

He watched her and wondered if she was the cougar that Mason had told him about today. He'd gone on and on about how she'd tamed the horses to the point where he wanted to beat his brother's head in. But the cat laying here now made him think that she might be a lot more fun than he'd thought. At least he hoped so.

"You must be Susan...I mean Susie, right?" He didn't know why, but he was disappointed when she didn't answer him. "I was tied up at work. I run the mill in town until they find someone to take it over. They said you were working off your punishment."

Gerard took a step toward her when she stood up. He felt someone behind him before she growled low in her throat. When he turned slowly, covering himself as he did so, he was relieved to see the local alpha, Patrick Sexton—Paddy to his friends—coming up behind him as a wolf. He turned back to the female to introduce her to him and found himself alone. His disappointment was profound. He let his cat take him and turned to Paddy.

*I'm sorry. I had no idea she was out here.* Gerard told him it was fine, but he needed a good run anyway. *She's moving along the river. If you hurry you can still catch her.*

*Why would I want to do that?* Several things came to mind about why he'd want to catch the cat, but he didn't voice them to his friend. *She's this woman who works for Mason. Not anyone I want to get tangled up with. Maybe a good lay, but nothing more than that. I don't need anyone in my life that is going to be here only for a few days.*

As they moved deeper into the forest, his thoughts kept going back to the woman. So when Paddy tackled him, catching him off guard, he told him he was going in. Paddy was still laughing when he told him good luck, and that she was still near the river. Gerard headed in that direction, telling himself that he only wanted to make sure she was all right.

He had no idea what he expected to find when he saw her again. Certainly not her floating on the river as naked as he was. Watching her, seeing her like this, Gerard thought of how long it had been since he'd been with a woman, and tried to convince himself that was why he was thinking of going into the water with her and seeing if she was as sexy as she looked from the shore. He had a feeling that she was even more beautiful.

When she sat up and stared at him, he let his cat go and stood as himself on the shore. She didn't come to the banks as he'd hoped she would. Nor did she swim away from him. He fisted his cock when it began to ache.

"Are you going to come like that?" His balls tightened to his body as he heard her voice. It was as beautiful as she was, and seemed to pour over him like her fingers would feel should she only touch him. "Do you care that I'm going to watch you do it?"

"No. If you'd like, you can come here and we can come together. I'd like nothing more than to come inside of you." Bold words, and ones that he'd never said to a woman, much less a stranger, before. "I want to taste you too. Come here for me."

"No. But if you come, I'll come out of the water and dress. I'm starting to get cold." He thought about telling her he'd warm her up, but she moved in the water enough that he could see her breasts again. Gerard wanted her now, and moved to the water's edge to go to her if she wasn't going to come to him. "You're supposed to come over there, while I watch you. I don't want to have to hurt you, but I will if you come any closer."

"I want to fuck you." She shook her head, but didn't move deeper into the middle of the river. "Come here, Susie, and let me fill you. I have no idea why, but the thought of fucking you has my cock hurting badly."

"You're not what I thought you'd be." He only nodded, his feet in the cold water now. "Don't do this. If you do then we'll both be fucked."

"Come here." He watched her and saw her indecision. She wanted him as badly as he did her. He could see that now, and when he fisted his cock again, he moaned loudly so she could hear him. "Come and take me in your mouth. Then I'll eat you. Christ, my cat wants to eat you as well."

"I don't want this."

He nodded and moved into the water to his knees. He knew this river almost as well as he did his room, but not this bank. He figured that if he went much further he'd be above his head, or on his ass from falling. When she started for the other shore, he felt his cat move along his skin. They were both aching to fuck this woman.

Gerard moaned when she turned her back to him and began swimming away. He nearly dove into the water to go after her, but he would never have made it. She was standing on the opposite shoreline when he begged her to stop.

"Come for me. I want to see you." He nodded to her and fisted his cock faster. Watching her body, her hands moving over it, he felt his balls tighten up again. She pulled on her nipples, cupped her breasts. Even as her fingers slid in and out of her pussy, faster and faster, he knew that she was going to come hard when he did. "I'm going to come with you. My pussy is hot enough to burn me."

"Christ." He came then, his cock spilling his cum in the water and all around him. He closed his eyes when his vision blurred, and when he opened them, his body aching for more, she was gone. "Mother fuck."

Gerard sat on the grassy bank, his body hurting to find the woman even though he'd come only seconds before. He looked along the shoreline in the hopes of seeing her again, even for a moment, but he didn't, and when he lay back on the grass, he felt his body sort of mellow out, and he closed his eyes again.

He'd never had an encounter like this before. Gerard, like his brothers, had never been without a woman, but this was different. She had been different. Even when he'd been a lot younger, women, even older ones, seemed to love having him around. He'd never dated anyone older than him and had his pick of sexual partners for as long as he could remember, but nothing had made him feel like this one had.

When Paddy entered his mind a few seconds later, Gerard got up and made his way back to the house. *You should know that she's found her way back to the Mitchell ranch. I think she might be planning to sleep there rather than with you.* Gerard told him to fuck off, and Paddy only laughed as he continued. *You should have gone to get her, young Gerard. Playing with a mate like that will only cause you both heartache.*

He stopped moving and stood as still as stone. *What do you mean, mates? We're not mates. Are we?*

*I would think she knows what you are to her. Maybe you're a little slower, but had you gotten close enough — and I'm only assuming here that you didn't — you would have figured it out too. Perhaps that's why she ran from you.* He asked Paddy how he could locate her. *Yesterday. At the station. She killed one of my men, and I took a bit of her blood. If she causes me any more grief, which I don't think she will, then I will be able to hunt her down and tear her throat out. But as I said, I don't think that will be an issue.*

Gerard looked back to where he'd come from. She'd known that...he thought about her words now, and wanted to hunt her down and demand for her to tell him why she'd done that to them. Done that to *him*. They were fucking mates. Then Paddy laughed again.

*I'm not sure that you're mates, Gerard. You'd have to get close enough to her to find out for sure. And as upset as I'd say she is right now, I'd wait to find out. She would hurt you, I think.* He asked him how he knew she was upset. *Because she's cursing a blue streak at the wood that she's chopping. And the ax that she's using is very sharp. So if I were you, I'd not plan any more outings with the young cat. She will hurt you. But if it makes you feel any better, I have others watching over her. Though I have no doubt that she can take care of herself.*

*That's no reason why you should think she's my mate. I mean....* Then something occurred to him. *You can hear her. What's she saying? I never touched her, if that's what she's telling you.*

*No, you didn't, and that's not what she's saying. I'm close enough to her to hear her words. She is saying that she no more wants you in her life than you'll want her when you figure out things about her. I'm assuming that she has a checkered past that might concern you.* Gerard said that it wouldn't matter to him if she'd murdered someone. *Then, my young friend, I suggest you talk to your brother or Palmer Snow. They might enlighten you on a few things about her. From what Mason told me today, she has a bit of a history.*

*What sort of history?* Gerard made his way into the house. He didn't want to wake the house up so he didn't even bother going to the refrigerator, even though he was starving. *You know something. Please tell me.*

*I really don't know anything. But for what she did for me yesterday, I feel a little more protective of her than I would another stranger. Had she not stepped in when she did, Emma would have been hurt badly, and it would have been my fault entirely.* Gerard had forgotten about her killing one of his men. *Had she not done what she had, then, as I said, he might have caused me more pain than his death has already. I got a heads up, something that will save me a great deal of trouble when his family comes to collect his body.*

*So, you don't know for sure she's my mate. You don't know anything about her past, and you think she might have saved you some trouble. What is it you do know?* He wanted Paddy to laugh again and tell him it was all a joke, but Gerard knew that is was true. All of it. *Paddy, I'm not ready for this. I'm the baby of the family. The rest of them, my brothers, they should be mated before me.*

*You're a grown man, Gerard, and you should be happy that you have a mate, not complain that you're not ready. When are any of us ready for major changes in life? But I will tell you what I do know about her.* Gerard waited for him to speak, and when he didn't, he thought the man was just playing with him again. *Get to the Mitchell ranch now. There's trouble.*

Gerard turned and moved to the yard, and shifted immediately. He was running to the house even as he smelled the smoke. Terror like he'd never felt ran over his body, and he just knew she was dead.

~~~

Susie sat in the back of the ambulance without talking. She wasn't really sure what she could say that she hadn't already said. Someone had come up to the house just as she was going to bed. The smell of gas alerted her that something was wrong, and she'd gone to check it out. When she'd hit him from behind, the light in his hands had hit the wood pile and it had caught fire immediately. She knew it was because of the gas, but it didn't stop her from trying to put it out as he ran from the scene. She looked down at her burnt hands and wondered if anyone would believe her if she told them she'd tried to put it out as best she could. She looked up when someone said her name.

"You should go and shift." The man in front of her was one of the brothers, but for the life of her she couldn't remember his name. "It's Darin. You and I met today in the house."

"No, thank you." Looking around the small place, she looked at him again. "Are they taking me to jail soon? I have to make sure my things are with me. It's all I have."

"You're not going to jail. Why would you think that?" Nodding but not answering him, she looked at her hands. "My brother would like to speak to you. He's having a hard time with his cat right now, and he'd have better control if you'd let him see you."

"I don't want to see anyone. If it's Mason, tell him…I don't know what to tell him." He didn't say anything, and she looked up at him. "I think there's a chance that I'm a mate to someone from around here. I don't know who it is, but I'd like to be left alone. Do you think that Mason could let me go early? I'd like to run now."

He smiled at her then, and she felt her own smile start to curve up. It wasn't like her to enjoy talking so much. And when he told her he'd be back, she felt the loss of his closeness. Closing her eyes, trying her best to ignore the smallness of the bed and back of the ambulance she was in, she nearly screamed when someone touched her leg.

"You." He nodded. The man from earlier was moving into the small space even as she tried to wrap her mind around what he was doing there. "You should go away and not touch me. I'm going to go to jail soon, and there will be no coming together for us."

"You ran from me today." Not bothering to deny or agree with him, she tossed off the blanket that someone had put over her and heard his hiss of breath before she realized what he might be seeing. "Why haven't you shifted and taken care of these wounds? Is this their doing? The men that are supposed to be caring for you? Damn it all to—"

"I would like to go now if they're going to take me in." He moved to touch her leg where the worst burn had happened. "Don't touch me. It'll hurt and I don't want you to touch me."

"Hush." Susie watched as he ran his finger along the biggest burn. His fingers were warm, but the pain was still there. "You should shift and heal, or I could do it for you. Taste all of you."

Her body was responding to him touching her, and to his words. She knew that he could smell her; hell, she could smell him too. When he ran his fingers down her cheek to her lips, Susie moaned, then begged him to leave her alone.

"I can't, and you know that. And I think you know that it's too late for the two of us now." Nodding once, she moaned as his mouth moved over the same area where his fingers had been on her face. "I want to kiss you. Taste to see if you're as delicious as I think you're going to be."

"I'm an ex-con." That had him pausing enough that she could force herself to move back. "They said I killed some people, and I went to prison for it."

"But you didn't." She didn't say anything, but he seemed to know what happened as he leaned away from her but held onto her hand. "You were recently released. The man that had killed those people is in jail now, and you've been set free. You're no more an ex-con than I am. You were exonerated, and now you're working for my brother because you saved his wife yesterday. I've been talking to my brother."

"I'm not like you." He asked her what she thought was different about them other than them being man and woman. "You have money to burn. You have a life, a job, and a family. I have a bastard of a father, a dead mother, and five years of my life gone because someone didn't check the facts like they should have."

"No, not all true, but some. I don't have any money other than what I get paid each week to work on the ranch and the extra I'm getting for running the mill. Both my parents were killed when I was five, so I didn't know them that well, but I do miss them. But if you understand that I'm your mate then you have to also understand what that means for us. I'm not going to leave you. And I'm not going to let you leave me." Susie looked out at the cruisers that had arrived not long after she'd fallen away from the smoking wood. "You knew what I was to you when we were in the woods earlier."

"So? It wasn't like you were thrilled about meeting me either. You just wanted a fuck. And you weren't even caring if it was any good for me." When he didn't answer her, she knew that she was right. Then he frowned.

"Do you really think that...? Well, obviously you do. I never leave a woman unsatisfied. Ever. And when this is done, I'll show you just how thorough I can be." She snorted, and could see that he wasn't any happier with her than she was with him. "We really need to talk."

Susie looked away from him. She didn't have any idea what was going to happen to her now. They were going to take her in, this much she knew. First of all, she'd been staying in a house that wasn't hers. Trespassing on the land was a big deal. There was no proof that there was a man that started the fire, and as far as they knew, she was nothing more than a woman without any means of supporting herself. Which, she supposed, was true. And now she had this man in her life. She looked at him when he said nothing.

"I don't care for people." He only nodded at her. "You have this big family that is going to expect you to find someone more suited to what you are, rich and fabulous. What do you think you're going to do with this thing that might or might not happen between us when I'm taken back to jail?"

"I doubt very much my family would care if you really were an ex-con, or that you had twenty-five children somewhere in your background." He knew as well as she did that there would have been no children of any union she'd had before he had come into her life. Her body had been waiting for him. "What do you mean, taking you back to jail? Is that what you think? That you're going to jail for this?"

"Yes." Susie felt tears in her eyes. "I don't want to go back to prison. I didn't do well there the first time, and I won't survive it again."

"You're not going anywhere." She pulled back from him when he tried to pull her to him. "Let me hold you, Susie. Then I'll go and figure this out and take you home...take you somewhere."

He held her for several minutes, and as much as she hated to admit it, it did feel really good for someone to hold her without it being violent. The only time in her life she could remember being held was to be punched, or sometimes tied up by her father.

After Gerard left her, she tried to think what she had to do now. Getting as far from the man as she could was her best bet. But even as she made her way to the doorway of the ambulance, she knew it was going to be harder than she'd thought. The woman standing there looking at her made Susie stop moving.

"He said you'd run. I didn't believe him, of course, but he was right." Susie looked around to see who was close. "You can try and get away, but I'll find you. Do you know who I am?"

"The alpha's bitch. The wolf." The woman nodded. "I didn't want to have to kill that other wolf, but he was going for the leap bitch. He attacked first."

"So I heard. And now my husband and I wish to make you welcome into the pack, as you are in the leap." Susie stood up now, the pain almost bearable. "You can't leave him. Do you know what will happen should you leave him now that he's found you?"

"Do you know what will happen to him when my father finds him? Or me for that matter? He wants something from me that I have no desire to share with him. My father, I mean." The woman shrugged. "He's a bastard and a prick, and will stop at nothing to get me working for him again."

"Work how?"

Susie didn't answer but moved to where the men were standing around the yellow tape. She had missed something earlier when they had pulled her off the smoldering fire, and she wanted to have another look. As she made her way to them, limping heavily, she thought about several things, mostly the man that had tried to burn the house down around her. He'd run off before she could tackle him. Putting out the fire had been much more important to her than chasing a man she had already gotten a scent of.

When Gerard came up behind her, she didn't look at him but at the burnt wood. "What are we missing?" She looked at him and said she didn't start the fire. "We know that. But he left nothing behind to help us. No scent. No prints. What is it we're missing? You were the only one here with him, so tell us what you remember."

She moved to the tape, then looked at the cop standing there. When he lifted it up for her, she moved to where he'd been standing. It placed her about where the man had been that had tried to burn the house down around her head.

The man had poured the gas on the wood that had been stacked for the fireplace. "I was in the back bedroom just getting ready for bed. The room that falls out into the woods, so I'm assuming it was the master suite. I could smell it. The gas. It was powerful." She looked back that way and thought of something. "I don't think I could have smelled it from here, do you?"

Mason sent someone around the house to see if there was more gas there. Susie looked down at the grass, then knelt down onto it. She looked to her right and thought of something she'd not remembered until then.

"There was another man. He was about fifty yards that way." She pointed out toward where the garage was. "I didn't really see him, but he...a bright light, like a cigarette, was burning in his hand too. I saw it go to his mouth where it brightened when he drew on it. This man, the one that set the fire, he smelled of it too...of the cigarettes that the other man had. But more of an association smell rather than that he smoked too. Or maybe not nearly as much I think."

This time the officer with them spoke. "Send three men out there to see if they can find where he might have dropped a butt. Look for footprints too. And take one of the Douglas men. Have them...you know, work their kind of magic and see if they can sniff something out."

He meant shift. Susie might have suggested that they take one of the wolves, but had no idea whether there was much of a difference in their ability to sniff things out or not. Instead she stood up and looked around.

"When I came around from behind him, he didn't turn at all to see me. He was human, so might not have heard me like a shifter would have. Also, he was burned. I kind of pushed him into the flames. Had he not smothered some of it, I might not have been able to put it out as easily." Mason asked her if she had his scent. "Yes. In addition to the cigarette smell, he smelled of bear and drugs. The nonprescription kind."

# CHAPTER 4

Gerard watched Susie. She was hurting, all of them could see that, but she remained calm and answered all their questions every time someone asked. He wanted to make her shift and take care of her burns, but he figured she was going to do it when she wanted and not before. He had to smile; she was as stubborn as he'd been told she was. When she came toward him after going over what she'd found and seen again, Mason did as well. As they met near him, he reached out and carefully pulled her into his arms. He was happy when she didn't fight him, but he was also worried that she didn't.

"I have a favor to ask you." Mason didn't look at him when he asked Susie, but Gerard felt her stiffen. "You can tell me no if you don't want to do it. It's not that big a deal, really."

"You mean I can tell you no, but you'll find some sort of punishment to make me do it anyway, right? Well, I can't give you the winning horses. Not that I can't, but I won't." Mason did look at him then, and Gerard could see his confusion. Then he looked back at Susie. "And if you make me do that—because I'm pretty sure you know that you can—I will hurt you. I know it would mean my death, but I don't really give a shit what happens to me again so long as I don't have to be cooped up again."

"I don't need you to tell me the winning horses, but it's nice to know that you won't do it. And as for you always assuming that someone wants you to do something nefarious or illegal, that's not the way I work. I wanted you to help me with the cattle that we have on the property. They're skittish too. And there are a couple of horses that I mentioned to you this morning that I'd like to make sure are all right. Christ, you need to chill out."

Susie pulled away from Gerard, and before he could pull her back, Mason reached for her. It was over in a second. Mason was on the ground and Susie had a knife at his throat. He wasn't sure who was more surprised by the move, Mason or him. But Susie was as calm as she was about most things she did or said.

"Don't grab me." Mason nodded but didn't speak. "I...I should sit you down and...don't hurt me please. I will explain, but I want to leave here in one piece."

"Your father?" She nodded at Mason. "I shouldn't have grabbed you. I know better. My mother raised me to be gentler to women, and even though you can more than likely kick my ass, I should know better anyway. Can you let me up?"

When she was off him, Mason didn't stand but sat on the ground. Jace and Darin came to him, but he stopped them with a raised hand, telling them that she didn't do anything to him that he didn't deserve.

"I would appreciate it if you'd help me with the rest of the cattle on this ranch. They have been sorely abused. Not so much with the whip that he used on the horses, but with other things. I think a few of them will have to be put down." Susie looked at Gerard, then back at Mason as he continued. "There is also an issue with a few of the other horses. I'm not sure where they might have come from, but they're not branded and they won't come near any of us because of what we are. I want to help them if we can. And if not, then figure out what to do about them in the long term."

"Cougar, you mean." Mason nodded at her. "And you don't want anything else done with them? You don't want me to convince them that they can do things that they're not bred for?"

"Can you do that?" She didn't answer him. "No. We don't want them to go beyond what they were intended for. But I would like to talk to you about what you can and can't do. Purely on a curiosity thing."

"I can sort of calm animals. I can't usually talk to them, but I can touch their mind and give them an idea. I don't want to do it. Not ever again. Also, I can...I can feel them. Their pain and emotions. They can...the stronger ones can communicate with me in the form of pictures or thoughts. It will get me killed if you tell anyone." Mason said he'd not ask her to, and if anyone did, he wanted to know. "I don't care for people. Not in any kind of form. I would prefer...if you'd allow me to—let me leave when I help you."

"You and Gerard are mates. And if you leave, he will as well. I know that you're running from your father. I can understand that completely, but looking over your shoulder for the rest of your life isn't going to make you any happier than you are right now. If you stay here, we'll protect you." Susie said nothing. "I found out some things about him. I'm sure you know most of it, but did you know that your father was a leader at one time?"

"Yes." Gerard wasn't surprised when she didn't give any more information. She wasn't being rude, he was sure about that, but it was more than likely a part of her upbringing. "I'll help you with your cattle and the horses. Should you...I should like to give you a name of a person who can buy them should you wish to sell. Or he will sell you some prime flesh as well. He's an honest man."

"Thank you." Mason stood up and looked at the abandoned ranch house before looking at Gerard. "I have another favor to ask. Not anything to do with the animals or anything like that, but.... Can the two of you stay here? I mean, until we sell? If we sell? I'll make sure that the pantries are filled and you have what you need in the way of linens. Holly and Emma have already stripped all of the things from the house that were no good. The rest...I think it's being washed up now. I'd just feel better knowing that someone was here all the time after this."

Gerard said that he would, but he'd have to talk to Susie. When Mason stepped away, thanking Susie once again, Gerard followed her into the house. She sat down on the sheet-covered couch.

"I don't want to be here long term, Gerard. He'll come, and what happened tonight will be very small in comparison. Nor should I be your mate." He sat down. His cat was pissed off and wanting to mark her now, but Gerard wasn't going to hurt her, any more than she'd already been hurt, by forcing her hand. "I'm not like you."

"You said that before. I'm not any closer to knowing what you mean by that now than I was then. How are we not alike? Is it the money? Because I don't have any, as I've said. I work for what I have. My brothers married into money, but I don't have any."

"You could if you waited for someone else to come along. They might not be your mate, but you'll be better off with them." He said nothing. "I know that it doesn't work that way, but you have no idea what kind of person I am."

"No. I don't. And you don't know what kind of person I am either. I'm not a bad person. I work hard. Lately I've been running the mill to get it set up for the town. And I found that I enjoy it very much. I can talk to people with the same interests as me. While my brothers and I are on the same page so far as ranching, these people aren't related to me." She said nothing, and he liked the way she wasn't someone who had to beat her view into a conversation. "I went to high school and did all right. Played some ball for a while, but didn't care for that since I had to keep holding myself back all the time. Took some of the enjoyment out of it when I was stressing about hurting someone because I was stronger. But it did teach me a few things about sportsmanship, as well as rules need to be followed. I want to be with you. My cat needs to be with you too, Susie."

"My mother robbed a store with some of her friends. They shot and killed a young man behind the counter when he wouldn't give her the combination to the safe in the office, as well as some of the customers." He hadn't known that, but it mattered little to him what her parents had been like. Susie was the only one that mattered to him. "My father was arrested and served time for armed robbery too. No one was killed that time, but he did a nice walk in prison for it. I was there as well."

"You were accused of killing some people in their car." She nodded and got up and started pulling the sheets off the couch and chairs. To him it said they were staying. "Do you know why you were arrested?"

"I didn't at the time, but I have since found out that my father set me up. He had it in his head that I'd be sent to the same place he was so he could pull me under his wing. Sort of protect me. Really it was to use me and what I can do. I'm not sure what he thought I'd do for him in there that I didn't want to do for him on the outside, but he did it to me." She laughed bitterly. "He didn't take care of me when I was a kid other than to knock me around all the time, so I wasn't really sure how that was going to work. But I was sent to a woman's facility, while he was in an all-male place. My parents are not the smartest cats in the world."

By the time they were in the kitchen uncovering things, she'd gotten quiet again. It was kind of calming, but quiet, like a peaceful walk in the woods or a stream running over rocks. As they looked around at the pantry, he realized that someone had stocked it with things they'd been eating while working there. He found a pad of paper and began making notes on other things they'd need. Mostly it was meat, but he did add eggs and bread to the list too. When he moved to the refrigerator, he watched Susie as she sat at the table and added things to the list as well.

"I can cook, but not anything fancy." He noticed that she didn't look at him when she talked about herself. "I can read a recipe and make things that way, but I don't know how to make things from the cuff."

"My aunt can. But then she's been cooking for a long time." Susie nodded. "Can you look at me please?"

It took her several seconds to do as he wanted. And when she did, he could see the struggle she was having with something. He didn't ask her what it was, but he had an idea it was all of the shit that was going on, on top of what they were going through. He moved to the table and sat across from her before speaking again.

"I won't hurt you. You know that. Nor will I make you do anything you don't want." She nodded again and lowered her head. He lifted her chin to look at her again.

"Susie, you can trust me and my family to keep you safe. I swear to you, your father won't get to come near you."

"He will as long as…if we mate, then he no longer has control over me, right?" Gerard had forgotten about that rule of their kind. So long as she was unmated, her father could make her do things that she didn't want, and he could treat her anyway that he wanted. "I'm so tired of running, Gerard. I don't want you to get hurt, but I want to stay here."

"Then we have to…I don't want to rush you, but when you're ready, we'll mate and bond. It's not why I want you, but it will go a long way to keeping you safe from him." She nodded, but only sat there. Gerard knew that he should be getting ready to go to work today. The ranch needed a great deal of work and time, but he also knew that the two of them needed something too. "I have to run into town to get some supplies for us. And to go by my brother's house to get the linens he was talking about. I don't know about you, but I'm too stressed to sleep now. Would you like to go into town with me? Get some breakfast at the diner?"

"You want me to go with you?" She seemed so surprised that he grinned. "I don't have anything nice to wear. Just what I have on and one more pair of pants."

"We can take care of that too if you want." She said she had some money. "I do as well…not a great deal, but a little bit put away. We'll split things down the middle for now. I don't know what sort of job you want to have, but I get paid well for working for the RA, the Ranchers Association. Also, I work the mill when I can. It's going to open in a week."

"I need to find a paying job too."

He thought for sure that Mason was going to pay her for helping them out, but didn't say anything. He had no idea what sort of arrangement they had and didn't want to step on toes. Right now anyway. As they finished up the list, going from room to room to see what they might need, Gerard told his brother what they were going to do.

*You should buy the farm, the two of you.* Gerard told him he didn't have that sort of money and more than likely never would. *We don't own it now, the RA does. And I'm betting we can come to some sort of arrangement until you get your feet under you. Maybe even rent it to you for a little while if you want.*

*I'll have to talk to Susie. She might not want to live here. I'm not sure where we can live to be honest, but we're taking it sort of slow.* He asked Mason about the parental law concerning daughters. *She said that he rules her and she'll be free when we bond. I'm not sure I want that to be the only reason we do this, but it would help her, right?*

*I have no idea. I've heard of the law before, but it's old. I didn't even know that it was still practiced anymore. I certainly never would use that.* He told him he thought that Ernie Benjamin would use whatever he could to control his daughter. *You might be right on that. And I wouldn't put it past him to know that he was making rules up as he went along. She didn't know a great many things that she should know, being a full blood. And not knowing to report to me is a biggy.*

As soon as Susie came into the room, her hair brushed and pulled back into a ponytail, he moved to her to kiss her. Gerard wanted to sit her on the counter and take her, but he really did want to take this slowly. Kissing her on the mouth gently, he took her hand and led her to his truck. This was going to be fun, he thought. Gerard had never been grocery shopping before other than to pick up a few things for Aunt Georgie, and wondered how it was done. He supposed they'd find out together.

~~~

Georgie watched Gerard and Susie shop. Every time Gerard would put something in the cart that wasn't on their list, Susie would put it back without a word. Then she realized that he was doing in on purpose. Making her huff at him when he didn't follow the list he'd made for them. As Georgie came around the next corner and in front of them this time, Gerard was being reprimanded for putting cereal in the cart. He no more ate that stuff than she did.

"Ask her." Georgie had to fight hard to keep the smile from her face when Gerard kissed her on the cheek before turning to Susie again. "Ask my aunt how much flour we need for a week or so."

"Do you bake?" Gerard nodded and Susie shook her head. "Are you planning to divide the chores at the house? Like the baking and then the cooking? It might help me answer you if I know that."

"I don't bake. I can cook, but not anything complicated." Georgie would bet her last nickel that Susie could make anything if she set her mind to it. "Cookies maybe, if it's not too hot outside. But if I had to make bread, I'd be lost."

"I can make bread. Aunt Georgie showed me how." Gerard noticed the look on Susie's face when she did. Like the girl wasn't feeling inadequate enough right now. "Of course, I have no idea how to cook a pot roast. Not like the one you said you'd make for our dinner. I had no idea you had to sear it first."

Another lie, but Georgie loved him for it. When he winked at her, she wanted to hug him to her. Her baby nephew was all grown up. Georgie decided she could help them in ways she'd not been able to help the other girls.

"I have some of Gerard's mother's recipes. I can give those to you to follow. She liked to cook in a controlled way. Lay out each ingredient before she began, to make sure she had it all. Then measure each thing before she would mix it in the bowl. I bet you're that way too." Susie nodded at her like she'd thrown her a lifeline. "I have a few of them in my purse. Let me look."

Georgie unearthed three. They were earmarked for Holly, who wanted to make Jace macaroni and cheese sometime, and the other two had been for Emma. She handed them to Susie, who started sorting things in her cart to make sure she had what was needed. Georgie looked up at Gerard while he helped her.

He loved her. Georgie had to hold onto her cart when she realized that not only had he grown up, but he'd gone and fallen in love as well. When it was evident that they were going to need more things, something else occurred to her. They were on a tight budget. She had no idea why it had only just occurred to her that they needed more than what was in their cart, but she felt badly for not thinking of it earlier.

It was on the tip of her tongue to offer to pay for things. She wanted to hand over her credit card when she heard Susie tell him that she could get herself some clothing next time they came to town. And Gerard said he'd get his boots then as well.

The ranches were making money, and both Mason and Jace had married into money, but Gerard and Susie didn't have that. They were as poor as church mice, and they had nothing else to fall back on. They loved each other, that was evident, but it could be much easier on them if there was a little more in the coffers, she thought. When Emma reached out to her, she had to ask her to wait until she got some control over her emotions.

*Are you all right?* Georgie told her that she was, then in an abbreviated version, told her what she had just witnessed. *Oh. I never thought…. We have to do something.*

*I don't know what it would be. Susie is very…I'm thinking she'll be hurt if we just step in and take over. I think she's looking for work. I didn't know that Mason wasn't paying her for working the ranch for you guys.*

*He is. We all are. I'll talk to him. He might not have thought to tell her that he was paying her. And for that matter, Gerard too, for watching over the house for the RA. And if she's looking for a job, I might have one for her. Ed Clark is looking for someone to come into his new office and help out as a secretary. I don't know how much it pays, but I'm sure it will pay well.* Georgie reminded her that Susie didn't like people. *I'm sure that she doesn't, not the way she's been treated. But we can work something out. As for the ranch, Mason said that they're going to keep an eye on the Mitchell place for him. He also mentioned to them they should buy it. I guess I know now why Gerard turned him down.*

Georgie knew that Mason had asked them to watch the house so that nothing else happened to it. It had never occurred to her to think about money for them. While growing up, the boys had never had much and neither had she, but they had made due. Much like these two were doing. She knew that it wasn't her fault, but she did feel bad about what they'd had to give up to keep afloat for all these years.

*I'm going to give them some recipes and a few of my cookbooks. Susie said she can read one, and I think she'd feel better if she had a few she could follow.* She thought of something else. *I have so many gadgets at the ranch I can give her too. Measuring cups and whatnots. I have no idea if the Mitchells left any of that kind of thing behind.*

Emma told her that she'd get back with her. And by the time that Georgie was checking out, she had a plan. Not a big one, just a little one that would help them out, but she was excited to do it. Georgie put her things on the belt, along with a few extras. It was time to stock up the pantry over there again, and this time with things that a young couple could use, not things to feed grown men working in the field. She was thinking of gathering her friends up and having an old fashioned housewarming party for them.

Going home, Georgie drove her car carefully. About a month ago, Jace and Holly had gotten her a newer used car that had four wheel drive, and she was still slightly nervous about driving it. She'd tried to tell them that she didn't need it, but Holly pointed out that with the baby coming, they wanted her to be able to babysit for her when she wanted. It had been on the tip of her tongue to tell her that she'd watch the baby every day, but she held back. She didn't want to be too pushy with her first grandnephew or niece.

The car came out of nowhere. Georgie wasn't going fast, but the other car, a dark sedan, was. And when he ran her off the road and into a ditch, it was all she could do to control her cat. Georgie sat there for several minutes until she felt like she could talk without being hysterical before reaching for one of the boys.

As she got out of her car, the car that had driven her off the road pulled up beside her. A large man got out on the passenger side, so she got a good look at him. Pulling her phone out of her pocket, she took several pictures of him as he moved toward her. When she saw the gun, she felt her fear level shoot up and her cat get pissier.

The sound of an oncoming car had her looking in that direction when the man did. It was Gerard and Susie. She didn't want them to get hurt, but she'd never been so glad to see anyone in her life as she was them. As soon as the truck came to a stop, Susie shot out of the door and shifted in midair. The man ran to the car again and was getting in just as Susie got a hold of him. Her cat tore into the man's leg even as gravel shot up from the road when the driver peeled out. Georgie nearly fell into Gerard's arms when he reached for her.

"Are you hurt, Aunt Georgie?" She told him just scared. "Yeah, me too. What the fu…what the heck was he doing? Did he run you off the road?"

"No, I was wondering the same thing…what the fuck was he doing? And yes, he ran me off the road and into the ditch." Georgie was shaking so hard that when Gerard let her go to check on the car, she had to lean on his truck. Susie came to her and rubbed her head on her leg. "You probably saved me from getting shot, dear. I swear you looked like an avenging warrior coming after him like that."

"She told me to stay in the car in case he got away. I have never been so afraid in my life as when she jumped from the truck." Gerard came up the bank as he continued. "Mason and the rest of them are on their way. But I'm afraid your car is trashed. You were very lucky."

Running her fingers through Susie's fur while listening to her purr, Georgie thought she was indeed lucky. But she was a little afraid of what the boys would say when they got there. Then she felt slightly light headed, and heard her name being shouted as the blackness took her.

# CHAPTER 5

Gerard put the last of their food in the pantry and then turned to look at Susie. She'd been so quiet after they'd gotten his aunt loaded into Mason's car. Georgie had been all right...just the situation catching up with her, she told them. And everyone agreed that she would stay at Mason's for a few days, just to make sure she was all right. Palmer had even come over to sit with her when the two of them left.

"Are you hungry?" She shook her head, then nodded. Gerard laughed and went to her. "We could go into town and get a couple of burgers if you want. I know that the diner on Tenth has a pretty good one."

"I want you to make love to me." He felt his cock stretch, but he didn't touch her. She was in charge of this, and he wasn't going to take that away from her. Or at least he'd try not to take over. "I've had sex before, so you know, but it's never been that much...it's never been very fulfilling. I'm guessing that has to do with them not being my mate."

"I would think that was some of it." He moved behind her and put his hands on the table on either side of her. He could smell her. She was aroused some, but not where he wanted her. Nuzzling her neck, he heard her heart rate pick up. "I've thought about lifting you up to the counter and taking you that way so many times it's hard for me to come into this room without hunting you down. Or against the wall. Either of those sound pretty good to me."

"What about the bed?" He told her that could be for later. "You don't want to go there and have sex? I mean, in the room?"

"I'll go where you want me to, but the thought of taking you here, hearing you scream out your release, that sounds very good too." Gerard kissed her shoulder, then moved his mouth along her neck to her spine. "Your skin tastes like sweet chocolate to me. I'm betting your juices are even better."

"Gerard, we should go to the bedroom." Her husky voice had him turning her on the chair and lifting her to the table. It was almost the right height for what he had in mind, and he lifted her hips up to bring her closer to his cock. "You're hard. And thick. When I saw you coming at the river, all I could think about was how much I wanted to feel your cum burn on my skin."

Kissing her now, her lips were warm and wet from her tongue. Suckling her lower lip into his mouth, he watched her eyes as they darkened with need as she wrapped her legs around his thighs. Rocking into her heat, he lifted her blouse up and over her head, then dropped it to the floor as she began to unbutton his flannel shirt. As her fingers moved over his nipples, Gerard cupped her bare breast in his hand and thumbed her nipple until it was as hard as his cock.

"I want to suck on you." He leaned back to let her do as she wished to him. Her hot mouth over his nipple had him curling his fingers in her hair and holding her to him as she nipped and sucked. He cupped her ass with his free hand and fucked her this way while she feasted on him. When she lifted her head, he told her it was his turn.

Her breasts were larger than he'd thought. Her blouse, seemingly a couple of sizes too big, had held their bounty in secret for him. When he leaned to her, taking only the tip into his mouth, he nipped hard enough to draw blood and sucked the tiny wound just to have her crying out.

The table was just about big enough for what he had in mind. Laying her back over it, he moved the salt and pepper shakers to the floor to keep them safe. With her blouse opened and her bra up over her breasts, he wanted to fuck her this way. Needed to. He unsnapped her jeans, mindful of the fact that she had limited clothing right now.

"I'm going to eat you first." She moaned, and he nearly pulled the zipper free of her pants when she curled her toes around his cock. He started to rock into her foot when she sat up and kissed him. He wasn't going to make it. He knew for a fact when she wrapped her legs around his waist that he was going to be buried deep within her long before he ever got to taste her.

"Fuck me." He growled, his cat wanting what she did. To mark her, to fill her with his cum. Laying her back on the table, all niceties gone, he ripped her pants and panties from her and freed his cock. "Now, Gerard. Fuck me now."

He slammed forward, filling her with all that he had. Pulling free slightly, he growled again when she dug her nails into his back, drawing blood. As soon as he filled her again, she pulled his neck to her mouth and licked his pulse. When she bit him, he knew he was going to come. And as soon as she sank her canines into his flesh, he felt his cock explode inside of her.

KATHI S. BARTON

Fucking her through his climax, he held her to him as he lifted her up to his body. The need to take her hard, pound her, had him taking her to the floor. As soon as she touched the cold tile floor, Gerard fucked her again, his body seemingly not his own. And when he felt her tighten around him, her scream filling his mind, he bit down on her shoulder and felt the bones there break under his teeth.

"Again, Susie, come for me again." He watched her face as she bowed up from the floor. Her breathing stopped for several seconds; he could hear her heart stop as well before it raced forward. When she came this time, he came as well, his cock emptying into her twice before he knew that he could do nothing more.

Dropping over her, he tried to roll to his back, but there wasn't enough energy in him to even make an effort beyond hugging her to him. As he lay there, his heart pounding a hard beat, his body trying to catch up to it, he knew that he was in love with her, and would love her for the rest of their lives and beyond. Her fingers trailed down his back, then fell from his body. Lifting his head, he looked down at her and realized that she was asleep or unconscious. Gerard laid his head upon her breast and smiled for no other reason than he had a mate and he loved her.

When she stirred again but didn't wake, Gerard got up and pulled on a pair of pants that he'd been meaning to wash. Picking Susie up in his arms had him staggering a little. Not from her weight, which he thought was slight, but because she'd wrapped her arms around him and snuggled under his chin. He carried her to the back bedroom and laid her on the bed.

Sitting in the chair near the bed, he watched her sleep. Then, getting up and kissing her on the forehead, he made his way to the kitchen. He'd not realized how late it was until just then, and he knew that he was going to have to get to work soon. He pulled out the things to make French toast, which was the only thing he knew how to make well.

Susie joined him a few minutes after Zach showed up. She'd showered and put on fresh clothing, and he wanted to run his brother off and spend the day in bed with her, going over every inch of her delectable body.

"I have some news for you. Not great news, but news." He sipped his tea as he spoke. Zach smiled at Susie when she told him to keep it to himself until after they ate. "Okay, I can do that. But congratulations are in order, I guess. I'm happy for you both."

Susie said nothing, but Gerard thanked his brother. When he handed him a plate of food, Zach looked at him questioningly. Gerard only shook his head. She was quiet and thinking hard. Gerard was okay with that.

They ate with Zach doing most of the talking. When it came time to clean up, Susie told him she'd do it since he cooked. He made his way to the bedroom to take a shower. When he came back, dressed in yesterday's shirt, she asked him if he wanted her to go and pick up things from his house.

"Your aunt said she had some things to give us, and that she had some of your laundry done. I don't…there is no washer and dryer here." He hadn't noticed that and wondered how much that would cost to put in. She came to him and wrapped her arms around him. "There's not much here, is there?"

There really wasn't. He had some things in his room at his aunt's house…a desk he was going to bring over, his old bed and dresser. There was a table that had been left behind, but only three chairs. The washer and dryer, of course, was going to have to be top on their list of things to get, and there wasn't much in the way of linens. Just the things on the bed and a few towels that had been stuffed in the back of the closet.

The couch in the living room was worn out and had a nasty spring that would catch him in the balls if he wasn't careful. There wasn't a television, which really didn't bother either of them as they didn't watch much, and all he had in the way of a computer was the laptop that he'd had since he'd gotten out of high school. He felt his heart rate spike up a little when he thought of how much this was going to cost.

"We'll be fine. And your sister-in-law said she knows of a job I can do. It's working for Ed Clark. Do you know him?" He told her he did and that he was a nice man. "I have to go and find Mason first. He wants me to help him in the pasture today."

As he made his way out to the yard to start working, he wondered how she was going to get around. There was only his truck, and while he didn't mind her driving it around, the tires needed to be replaced and he knew there was a knocking sound coming from the engine now. He looked up when Jace said his name.

"What's got you stressed out?" He wanted to tell him, wanted to unload on his big brother something terrible, but he didn't. Jace would want to step in and make it right, and Gerard wanted to do this on his own.

"Nothing. Are we going to work on the barn today or finish up on the one from yesterday?" Jace stared at him, and Gerard felt himself squirm a little. "It's fine, Jace. It's just that we're starting fresh on stuff. We'll get it together."

They went to the barn that they'd been working on yesterday, and when the rest of them showed up, they began to split up so that they could get it done faster. By noon no one had heard from either Mason or Susie, but he knew she was all right. And when his aunt pulled in the drive with the other women, he could see that she'd been busy as well.

It took them nearly an hour to take all the boxes in. While they'd emptied out the car his aunt had arrived in, two more cars had shown up. They were all full of things like silverware, plates, much needed mugs, and napkins; kitchen ware such as pans and potholders; baking dishes, as well as toothpicks and spices. One lady had even brought them some things that she'd been meaning to sell off...lamps for the living room, and a chair that didn't match her things or theirs, but made a nice addition. Even things like toilet paper and paper towels had been bought for them. He was overwhelmed by it all, and hugged his aunt several times as the ladies helped by putting things away. Then the final truck pulled up and brought them the rest.

The pantry was stuffed with food, staples mostly, but some things that they'd had on their list yesterday that they'd had to put back. He knew it was from Holly and Emma...even his aunt had been a little surprised by how much was brought. But he knew that to fuss about it or to even say they didn't have to do it would upset all of them, so Gerard thanked them and kept his mouth shut on the rest.

Gerard was the luckiest man in the world. He just hoped that Susie would be just as happy with the help and not be upset about looking like a charity case, something that she'd told him she never wanted to be again. Christ, he loved her.

~~~

"So you can just sort of connect with them." Susie nodded. Mason had been irritated at that at first, her never answering him, but he realized after about an hour it was just the way she was. "And what is it you feel when you touch them? The connection is stronger?"

"Sometimes. It depends on the animal." He waited for more from her, but when she laid her head on the forehead of the mustang that he was concerned about, he watched her face. And when she smiled and looked at him, Mason felt...well, renewed. "Mason, what if I told you that there were more than just these six up here? That this male is worried for his harras, but he is willing to trust me with them?"

"How many more?" He was a little nervous about the way she moved toward him. He knew she wasn't going to hurt him, but he watched her all the same. When she told him to keep his cat calm and not to make any sudden moves, he felt his heartrate soar. And when he heard the thunder, he looked up at the sky. "You think it will rain?"

Her laughter caught him off guard, and when he looked at her to ask what was so funny, she was staring off in the distance. He looked too, and that was when he saw the dark cloud filling the sky behind the trees. She told him not to move again, and all he could do was nod. Because in that moment, he could see what the thunder actually was. And it had nothing to do with the weather.

There were hundreds of them, probably more like thousands. Horses of all colors and breeds running as a pack, a large harras of horses. And when the dark mustang that he'd brought Susie out here to see moved toward her, he experienced a kind of awe that Mason had never known before. Susie Douglas was spiritual.

The string of ponies were all prancing around as if they had not a care in the world when he realized she'd known they were coming. The rest of the harras were so beautiful that it took his breath away. To see so many wild horses at once had him wanting to pull out his phone and take pictures. When he reached for his phone to do that, Susie put her hand over his.

"They'll be spooked by the noise. For now, we can just enjoy them." He agreed with that, and asked her where they'd come from. "I don't think they came from any one place, but they've been together for a while now. And like you, this mustang is their boss, their leader. And before you ask, yes, he sort of told me."

They moved around them, careful of their feet when the ponies got too rambunctious. As he moved his hand gently along their flanks, he marveled at the fact that he was a cat and they seemed to have no problem with him. He looked up at Susie when she laughed again.

"They'll come with us if you feed them. He doesn't want to have to go another winter without making sure that his family is safe. Will you...can we take them to the ranch? At least for the winter?" He tried to think how he could feed them when all he had on him was a bottle or two of water and a single sandwich. "I mean feed them at the ranch. They'll come to you as a herd if you'll take care of them."

"You should do it." When she shook her head, he nodded. "The Mitchell ranch hasn't been a viable ranch for years, and I know that they raised horses at one time. This is more than I've ever seen on the place, but I think you and Gerard can make it work. You could sell them if you want. And I'm pretty sure that you would be able to train them in ways that no one else ever would. Christ, Susie, they already are accepting of us, and you've yet to do more for them than to touch their leader."

"What about Gerard? I think he has it in his head to raise cattle, as you are. What do you think he'll say about having horses on the ranch instead of cows?" Mason was sure that Gerard would love to get out from under the cattle business. He'd not had his heart in it for years, but he just smiled at Susie. "I don't think I like that look."

"If you take these horses back with you, you could sell enough of them to buy the ranch outright. We'd make you a good deal. There are a lot of hands around us, not just on our ranch but the others as well, that need work and would do an honest day's job for the two of you. You and Gerard could train them to accept other paranormals like us, ones that can't ever hope to ride a horse because of what they are." Mason was warming to the idea and felt his excitement for it growing. "The only reason I can ride the one I do is because he has been on our ranch as long as I have. The one you're on? You are on her because she let you. You are going to make a great deal of money with your talent. And I promise you, no one will ever know your secret. Ever."

She only stared at the herd. He didn't want to push her…okay, that wasn't true, but he did know that she'd come to this decision on her own. Or after talking it over with Gerard. When she told him she'd think about it, he told her they should head back. The harras followed right behind them.

"I don't think we should tell anyone what we're doing." She looked over at him after they'd gone about halfway back to the ranch. "I'd like to see their faces when we come up on the ranch with these guys. I mean, don't not talk to them, but don't tell them what we're doing."

"You're very strange." He only laughed. And Mason realized that they'd come together today, her and him. Maybe she didn't fully trust him as yet, but their relationship was a little friendlier.

Mason was surprised—even though when he thought about it, he shouldn't have been—by how the horses seemed to herd themselves. The mustang that had been up on the ridge first would ride with Susie for a bit, then drop back to the rest of the harras and see what they were about. If this had been cattle they were bringing in, it would have taken them a dozen men and they would have lost a couple on the way. He wasn't stupid enough to think all rides with horses would be this way, but he liked it all the same.

As they entered the main part of the ranch, he could see the trucks in the drive as well as several men standing outside the large barn. Mason wasn't worried, knowing that if anything was wrong, he would have been notified about it. He reached out to Gerard when he saw him come out of the barn.

*Open the gates, little brother. Your wife has brought you something huge.* When he just stood there staring at them, Mason could imagine what was going through his head. But they were getting close now and they had to have somewhere to put them. After telling him again to open the gate, several men went to the other corrals and opened them as well. And like the way they had come with them down the pasture, the horses moved into the paddocks like they'd done it every day for their entire life.

It was nearing midnight when they had a count. Not a perfect counting of them—there was simply too many of them—but enough to know that even if they sold them for a thousand apiece, Gerard and Susie were not going to have to worry about money again. And the other ranchers who had come to see the new harras had a lot of questions for the new owners.

"How many do you think you're going to have sold come morning?" Gerard looked at him, glassy eyed, and Mason patted him on the back. "You're going to be just fine. And you should talk to Susie about the house and what to do with the horses. I'm thinking that you two will have enough money to make a solid difference in your lives."

"Yeah, you keep saying that we're going to be fine. But right now, I don't see it. We have over six thousand horses here. Six thousand. How the hell am I going to feed them? I don't even have a good bed and couch." Mason wanted to tell him he could afford it now but didn't. "Do you have any idea how much the vet bills are going to be? Christ, I think...I'm going to be sick."

"Gerard?"

They both turned to look at Susie. She looked just as poleaxed as her mate did. Mason suddenly felt bad for what he'd done. He'd talked her into this, and when they'd gotten here, he'd convinced Gerard that it was a good idea as well. When the two of them walked away from him, holding hands, Mason went to find Jace and ask him if he'd been a fool.

"No. Not a fool, but it's going to take more work than just the two of them can handle, ever. The cattle that we have coming in, as well as the ones we have on the two ranches alone, are going to take more work than we have men for, much less letting some of them come here to help out." Mason asked if he thought they could sell some of them. "I don't think that's going to be a problem, but knowing how much, to whom they can sell them to, and what sort of paperwork is going to be needed to sell them is the real question. And not to mention, Susie might need to train a few of them too. They seemed to be fine around all of us, but is that because she's here? Will they run wild when they go to the new owners?"

Mason could see even more problems with this many horses. The barns weren't in the best of shape. There were a few downed fences along the way they'd come, and they had no idea if someone else had a claim over the horses or not. They'd been on their land, so he'd just brought them here. Mason realized he might have fucked up, and said as much to Jace.

"I don't think so. Palmer is looking into the legalities of the thing right now. By the way, he's flipping excited to be a part of this. Ground floor, he keeps calling it. Ed is coming over in the morning to have a talk with Gerard and Susie about their ownership of them. I'm thinking, and this is just me, we should sign the house over to them in good faith just so they have something they can call home for these horses. And I hope you don't mind, but I also asked him to see what the going price for prime horse flesh is right now." Mason nodded his thanks and told him he was probably right about the house too. "You did right, Mason. I wouldn't have done it, but I think you did the right thing. Even if they only manage to sell a third of them, they'll be able to afford to buy this place. Aunt Georgie said that they're hurting for money."

"How much are they hurting?" Jace told him what their aunt had said to him. "My first instinct is to buy them what they need and to give them money, but I don't think that'll work with them."

"Why not? Both you and I have enough, more than enough, and we can do this for them. I think we should." Mason shook his head and looked over at the couple in question. "They're not going to make it if we don't give them a hand up."

"I think they will. And these horses? I think we should let them decide what to do with them. Susie found them; they came to her." Jace asked him what he meant. "She asked me what I'd think if she told me there were more than the six we went there for...and here they came. Like they were waiting for someone to call to them. She said that she didn't do it, but I think she's like some sort of animal savant."

"Remember what she said to you when you asked her for help?" Mason had been thinking the same thing. "You think her father knows what she can do and that's why he wants her to come to him? So he can...Christ, you suppose he was having her tell him what horses were going to win and by how much? Isn't that what she said to you that day?"

"Yes, and I do. And now that we know what she can do, we're going to have to protect her with our lives. Whatever she can do, someone is going to want that information as well. And for more than just the horses." Mason thought of something else. "The people that come for the horses. We're going to have to come up with an idea on how we just happened to have them. Even if we were to say they were on the ranch, Mitchell's widow could claim a part of the money."

Mason stretched his arms above his head. He was suddenly too tired to think about anything else tonight. As he made his way to his truck and the rest of them theirs, he wondered if he should have told Susie that they'd come back to help with the horses in the morning. Leaving them out there for one more night wouldn't have hurt anyone, he supposed, as the barns were in not too bad of shape. It was too late now, of course, but he did worry about her and Gerard. He did tell his brother he'd see him in the morning, and felt bad about how stressed he looked.

Mason thought about his family all the way home. They were a great bunch, and he knew that if any of them were to know what kind of shape that Gerard was in, they'd step right in and help them. Then he laughed. He supposed his aunt had known and just fixed it. But it was a gentle kind of helping. Not really his style, but he did know that something had to be done…and soon. He might just let Emma handle it. She was nicer than he was anyway.

# CHAPTER 6

Ernie watched the news feed twice more before he got up and left the bar. The fucking bitch was giving away his hard work. Not that he'd had much to do with raising his daughter. Other than a few squirts of his cum into her mother, he'd been pretty absent from her life. Of course, she had come to live with him for a time, but that hadn't been much. Knocking her around, he discovered, had been about the only thing he'd enjoyed about having a kid. That was until he found out she could converse with the animals.

"Like a fucking Doctor Doolittle." Ernie had called her that too, a lot, when she'd tell him she didn't want to do her job anymore. And he was pretty sure that she'd lied to him on a few occasions too. Telling him that so and so horse was gonna win, and then they didn't even place. She said it wasn't her fault, but he knew that she was controlling them animals like he did her with his compulsion over her. Now she had this herd of them right there to sell.

The news people had said that it was a beautiful sight to see all those ponies together. He knew better. They went on about how those horses just started to come in, a few at a time. Some of them had been given to them by farmers who were just not able to care for them, and others still had been brought to the Douglas ranch, she'd told the camera person, by way of donation. Hearing that they were caring for them made the reporter's heart feel good.

"Bullshit." Susan had made them come to her, and he knew it. And not only that, she was going to make money off them ponies and think she wasn't going to give any to him. "Bullshit on that too, damn it."

Ernie decided that he wanted a little of that action and was going to get it. Making his way to the hotel he'd been in since they'd let him out of jail a week ago, he tried to think how the hell he was supposed to get out to where she was.

He didn't have a car...not that he knew how to drive anyway. When he and his wife had been together, she'd driven them everywhere, and Ernie had liked having his ass carted around. He never let Anna hold it over him that she could do something he couldn't. The one time she did start to hold that shit over him, he'd beaten her within an inch of her life. And being mates didn't save her ass either. He was the leader of their ambush. She never brought it up again.

The hotel he was staying in was kinda run down. Not that he tried to complain too much. It was free on the condition that he find a job soon. The state was paying for it, as well as making sure that he had some food. He'd never been so happy in his entire life to find out the halfway house he was supposed to be staying at was full. Now he was out on the state's dime, and he planned to suck that tit dry.

There were other conditions too, not that he'd bothered to figure them out. But now that his darling little piece of shit daughter had some money coming her way, he was going to go and have a talk with her. This was going to be a way better deal than the release money she'd been given when they found out he'd had his guy lie on her. The news had called her Susie Douglas, but he knew her when he saw her. Changing her name wasn't going to keep him from figuring out who she was. Not when they'd blasted her picture all over the fucking news.

Ernie sat down on his bed and thought about his dinner plans. He wasn't supposed to go in bars or even any kind of establishment that served liquor of any kind. Hell, he thought, what was a man supposed to do after a long day of not looking for a job? Grinning, he called the pizza place down the road again and told them who he was and what he wanted.

"Yeah, about that. You said that the state would give us a check when we called in your bill. They said that you weren't getting any kind of compensation on food that wasn't prepared on your own."

Ernie said he'd come down there and make it for them then. "But if I have to make my own damned pizza, I expect to get a nice discount. One you give me, but don't tell them state boys I'm getting. That way we both make out, don't you think?" The man on the phone said that wasn't going to work either. "Why the hell not? You want to follow them rules, and I'm just helping you out some. A man has to make a little on the side, or things don't seem right."

"You're not going to come here and make your own dinner. And I'm pretty sure that's not what they meant when they said that. You're to go and buy your food and cook it on your own. As it is right now, you owe me two hundred forty-two dollars and ten cents. And I'm pretty sure I'm not going to get that unless hell freezes over, am I? You are a piece of work, you fucking prick."

"Don't you be calling me names, now. And you're damned straight you ain't. Not with that sort of attitude, you ain't. Christ man, can't you cut me some slack? I'm outta work."

The man only hung up on him, telling Ernie in his parting comment to get a fucking job and stop living by stealing.

Ernie could remember a time when he'd been leader of an ambush and businesses would beg him to take their products. Of course, that might have been because he'd been robbing them blind. That was until they saw the narrow path he was leading them down. Bankruptcy and ruin, one man had called what he'd done to him by eating there nightly with his friends and not paying for a single thing. Hell, they didn't even have to tip the waitress if they didn't want, which was fairly often. The owner had shut down his restaurant and left town the next week. Back then, one woman would suck him off while another would let him eat their pussy at the same time. He'd only had to knock them around a bit to get them to do it, but he was the leader, not some pussy who paid for sex. He'd had it all. Drugs, money, and women. Then he'd met Anna.

She'd been something else, his mate. Gave as good as he dished out to her, and then some. There had been nights when he'd fuck her so hard she'd be bleeding. Then she'd pick up a heavy something or other and beat him to shit with it. She was a firecracker. He should have taken better care of her, made sure she had some money for her habit. And it was a strong one, her being what she was. He should have told her that robbing that convenience store at that time would surely get her in trouble. Being in another state on a job, he'd only been able to stand by and watch her life fall to shit without him. But the state had figured out that

Susan was his and he'd had to go and pick her up. They'd made him promises back then too…more money on his food card, prime housing, and she'd have her lunches for free as long as he maintained a good work ethic.

"Like I knew what the fuck that was." He knew the definition but not how to go about it. He was an ex-con, for fuck's sake. How was he supposed to get a fucking job? And not one that made him wear a polyester uniform and be bossed around by some snot-nosed kid that thought he was all that because he was the manager of a fucking burger place. When he'd tried to work at one of them places, he'd smelled like raw meat and dirty grease for hours after he'd gotten off work. One day working that shit had made him see the light. Robbery was the only way to get ahead in this world as far as he was concerned.

He had standards too, by God. And they didn't have him working in a fast food place. He ate there, he didn't fucking work there. *Not in this lifetime*, he thought.

He leaned back against the headboard and tried to think what he was gonna do now. There wasn't any way for him to get credit. His money was all gone, too. Ernie had spent it for the gun he'd had to have almost as soon as he'd been released. He wasn't supposed to have it, being a con and all, but he wanted it and had bought it. Nobody was going to tell him what to do.

There was the possibility that he could go out and stick a place up, or rob some shit that had more money than he did smarts, but that would require him to get up and move. And right now, Ernie was comfy right where he was. He kicked off his shoes and wiggled his toes. The hole in his sock made him laugh, but he only had the one pair. Life had to get better soon or he was gonna be naked, he thought.

The real money was in the fucking daughter, but figuring out how to get to her and get it, that was the question. He was her sire, as well as the one she answered to, and she'd better by God remember that. But she was slick, he'd give her that. Making sure she was put with him in the same prison had cost him, and it hadn't even worked out that way. All the work he'd put into her getting caught and all was wasted. Bitch.

The monitor on his ankle burned him, but he didn't give two shits. He hated to have it on him, someone knowing where he was all the fucking time, but it wasn't as bad as being at one of them halfway houses, and a damned sight better than being in prison again. So long as he was out and not in one of those monitored houses, he could put up with a little discomfort. And what did he care if they wasted their time by putting it on him? He knew for a fact that they didn't really monitor them. He'd been all over this city since he'd been out, and not one cop had come to ask him what he was doing.

He glanced over at the bag that his first and only purchase had come in. The gun, bought and paid for with money the state had given him when he'd been let out, was to make Susan do what she was told if she gave him any shit. And he was almost hoping she would try it.

Just before she'd run off when she'd been a kid, he'd beaten her. Maybe he had gone a little over the top with his fists, but his cat had wanted more, so he let him have a go at her too. Frowning, he remembered something else about that day, something that had made him not try to find her for a while. She'd healed.

As his daughter, there was no way she could heal herself after he applied his superiorness to her. Smiling, he knew that his cat was bigger and meaner than she'd ever be, and he was positive that so long as she lived, no male would ever get close enough to her to become her mate. She was pretty enough, he supposed, but she was weird. And men, especially ones he knew, did not go for weird. Then there was the added fact that he had final say over everything she did. She was his.

The phone ringing startled him. He knew that it could only be one person...his parole officer, or in this case reporter. Neither the guy he'd been dealing with in finding Susan nor the girl herself had his number, but he did have the burner number, the phone he'd picked up a week ago, to make his calls. Picking it up, he didn't say a word until the person on the other end either hung up or spoke first. He wasn't above playing petty games.

"Then I guess you don't want what I know." The man then hung up. He had no idea who it had been, and he felt a slight tremor of fear slide over his body. What did he want? And more so, how did he get this number? He'd been told that as long as he was staying here, there would be no giving out the number to anyone. And he hadn't given it out himself. Putting the phone in the cradle again, Ernie stared at it, willing it to ring again.

When it did an hour later, he snatched it up like it was going to save his life. This time he not only said hello, but gave his last name too. He didn't know what this person knew, but he had a feeling he was going to want it.

"No more fucking games." He told him no, no more games. "When I call, you'd better fucking answer or you'll be set out on the streets like the piece of shit that you are."

He wanted to tell the man to shut up, he wasn't shit, but he felt himself slide off the bed and onto the floor. Ernie put his head on the floor and closed his eyes, waiting for the man to tell him to expose his belly, the softest and the most vulnerable part of any shifter.

"No, sir. I won't. Next time, you'll not have any problems with me." Ernie laid still. He was really afraid to have a thought, he was so terrified. When the man laughed, he started to lift his head but stayed when the man spoke again.

"She's not going to come to you easily. And when she does, you'd be better off just listening to her and then walking away." Ernie asked him who. "Susan Douglas. Your daughter. Though how she came from you is beyond me. Listen to her or not, but you stay away from her."

"Her name ain't Douglas, it's Benjamin, like mine. And I can take her back any time I want. I'm her daddy." The man laughed again. "Who the fuck is this? You tell me right now, and I'm going to come to you and kick your fucking ass."

"I'm Mason Douglas, her brother-in-law as well as her leader. And come on and try it. I'm betting right now you're so close to pissing yourself that you're holding onto your dick." Ernie moved his hand from his cock and shook himself. No way the man knew what he was feeling. "Stay away from my leap, or you'll regret it for a very long time. And you have two days to get out of my territory or so help me, I'm going to make you pay in ways you can't even imagine. I am leader here and I fucking rule you."

The line went dead, but Ernie just held it to his ear. He didn't move, wasn't even sure that he could. Fear of something or someone bigger and meaner than him made him hold his bladder tight and clench up his ass. The man was stronger than Ernie had ever been, even in his hey-day. Christ almighty, he was fucked.

But the longer he lay there, the more his thoughts shifted in his mind. Someone had just threatened him. He, Ernest Benjamin, had been threatened by some dick that was going to get himself killed as soon as he saw him. It didn't matter to him that he'd been thinking of rolling over for the man. That didn't even come into the picture now. The fucker had threatened him, and that just wasn't right.

Getting up to see if anyone was lurking outside his room, he didn't see anybody, so he felt stronger for it. Not even the payphone across the way from him had anyone standing around watching. Of course, they might have left by now, but he'd find them, sure as he was standing there. He wasn't even sure that it worked.

But just as he was closing the curtain again, he saw him...the man he knew had been on the phone just now. And when he stretched, his arms going up over his head, his cowboy hat, of all things, moved back from his face, and Ernie knew a kind of fear that had not just his cock and balls tighten up, but his asshole seemed to crawl up inside of him again. Closing the curtain, he sat down in the chair and didn't move the rest of the night. That man was fucking huge.

~~~

Mason watched her pace. Well, pacing wasn't what Susie was doing so much as she was stomping hard back and forth in front of him. He did glance over at Gerard and knew he'd be no help. The man was in love with his mate, and he was glad for him. But he wasn't going to save him should she turn on him again.

"I only wanted to scare him some."

Susie stopped to glare at him before she started stomping her way across the kitchen floor again. He took the opportunity to look around the room while she worked out her being mad at him for calling her father, and could see that his aunt had made good on her promise to only give them things she didn't need.

There was the old tea maker that was dark with age. The plastic was so stained up with tea it was hard to tell if it was empty or not. The dishes in the drainer were the ones that had been used by him and his brothers when they were younger, and he could see chips on the edges from their clumsy hands. The electric mixer hadn't been new in probably twenty years, and he knew that the skillet on the stove, drying the only way cast iron could, had been his own mother's. When Mason heard Susie clear her throat, he looked at her.

"What did you hope to accomplish by talking to him? Did you know that he's this great leader? And that his word is the only one?" He wasn't sure if she was serious or not, and one look at Gerard made him think she really believed that, because he looked as shocked as he was. "He could have hurt you. What if he had? What do you think that would have made me feel like?"

"Right now? I'm thinking you'd be thrilled." He stood up when she looked like she was going to hurt him. "I'm sorry. I should have told you what I was going to do. But I saw him and I just wanted to…to scare him a little, that's all. I think I did, to be honest with you. Susie, he's not as big or as bad as you think he is."

"He's hurt me." That confession didn't really say it all, and he was pretty sure that she might not tell them even if he asked. "He's mean. And my father. I have to do what he says. If I don't…if I don't, he'll hurt me again."

"You're healed." She looked at him with confusion on her face. "You can't heal if a leader hurts you. Not if he does it with malice. You didn't know that either, did you?"

"He said I belonged to no one but him." Mason was beginning to see the picture now. Maybe not the entire one, but enough to know that this woman might as well have been newly turned for all she knew about what she was. "I don't want to have to go back to him. But now, thanks to you, he knows where I am. And he knows where you are too. What if he comes here, Mason? What if he tries to hurt you guys? He will. He's a terrible person."

Mason sat down and reached for his aunt. The women would be better at explaining things than he was, but he'd give it a try until they got there. Holly and Emma were coming as well, his aunt said. They had some shopping to do for the new couple.

"Look. I'm not just your brother-in-law now that you're mated to Gerard, but your leader, as you know. But I'm not the kind of...I don't think anyone is a leader like your father." When she sat down too, he felt a little better about talking to her. "He's not a good leader, nor is he a good man. Which I'm sure you know, but he kept things from you. Important information that he should have told you. He can no longer control you like he did when you were a child. He isn't your leader, nor is he able to control you with compulsion. His power over you was gone the moment you mated and bonded with Gerard and became a member of my leap. But since you said that he hurt you, I'm assuming that it was with his cat."

"He can't come near you again, love. I'd die before I'd let him, and I can tell you, it will never come to that. He isn't going to come near any of us." Gerard pulled her into his arms as he continued. "We're a couple now. Never again will he be able to control or to hurt you. You're stronger than he is because of the fact that we're together. Mason is a stronger cat because of his mate; Jace is as well.

95

Not just as a cat but as a human too. Your father is no match for us. Not even for you."

"He will kill me this time." Susie looked at him, and Mason felt like a real shit for doing this to her. When he'd come here to let them know that he'd talked to her father, he'd been bragging. He'd taken the man to the ground...nearly made him piss himself. Now he felt like a bastard. "Promise me you won't do this again. That you won't engage him unless you have to. He's not just a big cat, Mason, but one that doesn't play by your rules. Not anyone's. He's mean and slick. He won't play fair and he'll not do what you expect. He's a monster."

"I won't. I promise." He stood up and told her again that he'd never do this again. "But if he comes here and hurts anyone in my family, and that would include you, he's a dead man."

"I'll kill him myself if he hurts any of you."

Mason nodded and moved out of the house. It occurred to him that she'd not said she'd hurt him if he did anything to her, so he decided to keep a closer eye on her.

He was walking up to the last barn to be cleaned up when he saw Paddy as a man at the corner of the corral. His voice was low when he began talking.

"I need your help." Mason told him whatever it was, it was his. "I might have to...I have a problem in my pack. I don't know who it is yet, but someone has been coming in and taking our food supplies."

"Why?" Paddy told him he had no idea. "I mean, it's not like you couldn't go and buy more food, right?"

"Exactly. I think they're doing it to get someone else in trouble. Mainly my wife. She's in charge of the pantry. We don't use it often anymore because the pack—thanks in part to you and your family—has been working more and the income is helping a great many people. Two of the women have plans to open a shop in town, and your wife and sister-in-law have hired a few of the others to come and help out with various projects that they have going."

Mason knew this and was glad for it. He'd even hired on more of Paddy's men to help out around the ranches. It had taken little for them to get used to working with cats, them being wolf and all, but it had been working out great for all of them.

"What is it you want me to do? I'm kinda limited on my ability to send you some of my leap. I don't have all that many in it." But that was changing too. As of this morning, three new families had asked to live and work here. A lawyer, as well as a doctor, was among the new leap members. "You have a plan?"

"I do. I think that someone is selling the stuff to the local diner." Mason leaned against the fence when someone from the pack came out to help. He had noticed that Paddy had moved deeper into the barn now, and no one would be able to see him unless they entered it. "From what I understand, you and your wife are part owners. Is that right?"

Mason's wife and her family were wealthy. He supposed in turn he was as well, but he wasn't comfortable with it yet. He was sort of like Emma's dad, the laid back and don't mean nothing to me sort of rich. Not really, but that was what the town assumed he was. Inside, he was mush whenever money was mentioned. He could not wait for Katie and Landon to get back from their holiday so Landon could be the one that they went to for issues of the town and its residents.

"You want me to have someone go in and have a look around?" Paddy said he wouldn't have asked it if wasn't so important. "I understand. And I'm sure we can do something. I might even have Ed Clark go and have a look around. He's working on becoming one of the most overworked small town lawyers there ever was. But he'll do this for you."

After Paddy left him, he walked around the corral to see the horses. Since the news team had shown up yesterday afternoon, they'd had a lot of people asking about buying them. So far not one of the horses had a mark on them, and new foals were coming almost daily. The herd was a little bigger every day.

Ed came up beside him with his ever present handkerchief, mopping at his brow. His smile made Mason smile back.

"Hot, isn't it?" Mason only tipped his hat back and looked up at the sky. They were predicting snow over the next several days, and he was pretty sure it was only about forty out. "I have information on the ponies. You're not going to believe the people coming out of the woodwork to claim them. One lady even told me that she'd come out and tell me which was hers when I asked her about markings. Told me she had about fifty in her yard and now they were gone. She lives in a retirement apartment. One of those ones that have nothing more than a postage stamp size yard. But boy oh boy, she was spitting mad when I told her that wasn't going to cut it. Pretty lot, aren't they?"

"They are. Can they sell them?" Ed grinned. "I take that as a yes. Do you have any information on how much a prime stallion can go for nowadays?"

"Do I ever. I had no idea there was so much information to be had on horse flesh and the selling of it. I have to talk to the new owners, and I did as you asked and put the house and all the land in Gerard's and Susan's name. Good idea, that. I'll have to tell Jace when I see him. But I have several buyers that want to come out and cut the herd. Had to look that one up too. My my, it's a lot for this old man to take in. Cut the herd means they want a few of them cut from the whole, to buy them."

Another reason that Mason was glad for the lawyer coming into his leap. "How much do you think they're worth? Ball park." Another grin and no answer just yet. "You're going to make me hurt you, aren't you?"

"Nah, not that. But it is fun to know more than you for a change. On average, about three grand each. More if they show any kind of racing ability, and more than that if they're pretty. And yes, I did find out that looks can make the difference." Mason asked him if he was kidding. "No. I don't kid around when it comes to this amount of money. The buyers that I was telling you about? One is from a big farm in Kentucky, another from somewhere in Louisiana. And one is from a farm out west who wants to…let me see what he called it. Oh yes, he wants to beef up his own harras. That's a problem they can have with horses. Too much inbreeding can cause long-term issues like you've never heard of. I know that I hadn't."

Roughly eighteen million. His brother was going to shit. And Susie was going to…he looked at the house when a car pulled in, and realized it was his aunt and wife. Georgie's new ride was nice, and he was thrilled that Emma had convinced her she needed four-wheel drive out here on the ranches. He smiled when she walked by it and wiped at the dust. He didn't think she'd ever had a new car before.

"I'm going to see to Gerard and his mate. They can be…she's a mite on the stubborn side, isn't she?" Mason said he had no idea. "Well, wish me luck. I think I might need it. Oh, and if it's all the same to you, I'm not mentioning the land being theirs now. I think I'll let you do that talking. You can take her. Me and my old bones can't."

Mason called him a coward, and Ed just laughed. He was let into the house just as the women got completely out of the new SUV. He might have to think of getting one for himself if it rode as good as it looked.

After kissing them both on the cheek, then going for a better one from his wife, Mason went to the barn to get his horse. It was time to get to work, and as much as he wanted to go and see Gerard's face when Ed talked to him, he had to get to the McBride house and see that things were all right there. Mason was enjoying being a ranch baron, but there were times when he missed just being the Double Deuce.

# CHAPTER 7

Susie was putting away the last of the lunch dishes, trying her best not to think about what the nice lawyer had told them this morning. There was no way that he was telling them the truth. Not that she thought he was lying. It wasn't that, but it had to be a mistake. She looked up at Georgie when she came into the room with a basket of clean towels.

"I found these in the basement of the house. They're not new, but they'll work out until you can get better ones. I'm afraid that I didn't have time to run them through the washer." Nodding, Susie took them from her and went to the washer and dryer that had arrived that morning, a wedding present from Palmer Snow. She wasn't sure that it wasn't a ploy of some sort to get them new things, but she was glad for it. "Honey, are you all right?"

"Not really." She was sure that wasn't what the older woman had expected her to say, but to be honest, if Susie didn't talk to someone soon, she was going to bust. "Did you know that there are all kinds of rules that no one told me about? I'm sure that Mason had a good laugh over how much I didn't know."

"No, he feels badly for you." She knew that he did. And she wasn't sure that was any better than him making fun of her. "Tell me what's really bothering you. Is it us, me? Coming over here all the time and helping you out?"

"I don't know what I'm doing. And you're helping me." That was true. When Georgie touched her arm, she turned to the woman. "I'm so afraid that I'm going to mess up. I don't know anything about running a house. I had to read the instructions that came with the washer three times to know how to put the detergent in before I felt like I could do it without ruining our clothing. I don't know how to make tea that doesn't taste like I made it in a slop jar. And even less about working with a lawyer. Which I'm to start doing on Monday. I'm not whiney, but I'm so overwhelmed right now that I think if someone came to the door to threaten me, I'd feel better when I hurt them."

"Sit down, child." Susie did but she felt stupid. When a little box of cookies appeared in front of her, she tore open the package and ate three of them before Georgie came back with a cup of tea for them both. "You like sugar."

"Only when I'm nervous." To prove her point, she pulled out two more and ate them before she felt better. "I'm very sorry about this. You must think I'm a ninny. A word, by the way, that I've never used before but think is perfect for me."

"When I was told that I'd be taking care of my brother and his wife's children, I had grand plans for them. I was going to cook them a meal every day that would fill their little bellies up, keep a clean house, and make sure that they never regretted me coming to live with them. I could never have replaced Norman and Zelma. They were the best people in the world, and loved their sons more than life itself." Susie ate another cookie and wondered if her mother had ever cared about those things for her. "I came to the house and found it spotless, because Zelma made sure that the boys could fend for themselves. And Norman made sure his boys could run the ranch so that it wouldn't fall apart should he take a needed vacation. Even little Gerard, a wee little guy, could make his bed better than I could, and cleaned himself up in the shower like he'd been born to it. Meals were hectic and most of the time not fit to eat. When I cooked, that is. And for a while there, the only person regretting me was me. I was doing a horrible job."

"No." Georgie nodded and smiled. "They love you."

"They do and they did back then. But I was a novice at caring for them. I'd never even changed a diaper for them when they were babies, and now I was their only hope of staying together." Susie took the picture that Georgie handed her. "Mason was fifteen when their parents were killed, and Gerard, the youngest, was only five. He was my partner when the others went off to school, and I learned a great deal from him. How their mom had used the washer. Where the clean dishes went when they were done, as well as what kinds of foods the others liked and hated. He even showed me where the cookbook was that his mom had used. It took me nearly a year before I felt like I was going to make it, and still daily I find myself making small mistakes."

Susie looked around the kitchen, thinking about her own childhood and what her parents had done for her. Little to nothing really. There hadn't been any trees at Christmas. Most of the time one of them would be in jail on holidays. She couldn't remember a birthday where there had been a cupcake for her, much less a cake or card. Thanksgiving was just a day for her parents to steal what they could from parked cars, while she had to watch the people inside eat their stuffed turkeys and pies.

Susie looked at Georgie. "When I was about ten, my father was gone. I'm not sure if he was in jail or just gone, but my mother said she was going out to get some groceries. That in and of itself was something strange. I'd never seen her as much as step into a store unless it was to meet a drug dealer or to pay someone off." She didn't look at Georgie as she continued. "I saw it happen. I followed her to see if she was really going to get me something for my birthday. It had been a couple of days before, but I was curious. She met up with three other people. A man that I didn't know and two women that she usually got high with. They were all deadbeats, and one of the women had had her children taken from her when they were born because she was such a terrible person. All four of them went inside, and after getting a bunch of junk food, most of it just beer and liquor, my mother went to the counter and the other three spread out around the store, shoving other customers around and then hitting them when the time was right. My mother pulled a gun on the kid there and demanded that he give her everything that had been made that day. Not just what was in the drawer, but everything in the safe as well. He was nineteen. Working his way through college, doing nothing but working a job to buy books for school. She shot him when he told her, several times, that he didn't know the combination to the safe and that he had no way of getting into the drop place that was behind the counter. Then when he was down, she stood over him and shot him until the gun was empty before reloading and doing it again. The other people with her shot the other customers as well, and nine people ended up dead that day. And for what, I wonder."

A tissue was put in her hand, and she wiped at the tears she hadn't known were falling. Susie nodded her thanks and thought of the things that had happened that day that had changed her life. As she continued, she tore the tissue to shreds rather than look at the nicest woman she knew.

"He didn't deserve to die no more than I should have had her as a mother. And the money in the drawer was all he had. There wasn't much, I heard. Less than two hundred dollars. I called them. The police I mean. Walked to the payphone next to the store and called them and told them what had happened. I even gave the names of the people with her, and my mother's. I knew at that moment that I was never going to mean enough to her or anyone that would make them want to keep me safe. That if I was going to make it, and I was going to give it my best, I'd have to only rely on me and to never trust another person so long as I lived." She looked at Georgie then. "Then you guys came into my life and I realized this time that there are some good people in the world, and maybe, just maybe, someone might love me like I want to be loved. Thank you for that."

"I love you too, sweetheart. And so does the rest of the family." Susie nodded but didn't look up at her. It was too much. "Well, I need to get my bottom in gear. Holly and Emma are going with me to the mall, and I'll be by to pick you up in an hour. I won't take no for an answer."

When Susie looked up, she noticed that Gerard was standing in the doorway and she wondered how long he'd been there. When Georgie kissed him on the cheek, he told her he loved her as she left. He never moved when she started talking.

"She brought us over some more things. At this rate we'll be fully stocked with household things and never have to buy anything new." Gerard sat down next to her and took her hand into his. He asked her to tell him the rest of her story. "My mother knew that it was me that called the police on her that day. She saw me there, standing next to the phone booth, when they brought her out."

"Good for you." She frowned at him. "I'm serious. Had you not called them, they might have left the store and killed more people. As it was, you having them arrested there, there were witnesses to what they had done, the cops in this case, as well as the fact that she didn't go back and hurt you. She might have too." He grinned at her. "You're very smart, my dearest love."

"You're supposed to be appalled by this, not nice about it." He asked her why. Instead of answering him, she got up to go to the bedroom to finish things up in there. Gerard followed and pulled her around to face him, and she felt her cat run along her skin. "You're supposed to hate me."

"I love you." She stared at him. He pulled her body to his, and his long lean body felt good against her. "I love you very much. The way you smell, the way you feel. I love the way you scream when you come. The little noises you make when your body is responding to what I'm doing to you. I love the way you try hard to make tea, and the way you tossed out the eggs this morning when you burnt them. You're doing your best to be better, and even though I could care less if you burnt the entire dozen eggs before I eat, I'm thrilled to death that you are here with me."

Susie moaned when he cupped her ass and brought her to his cock. It was on the tip of her tongue to tell him she had work to do and so did he, but he started nibbling on her neck and rocking into her as he held her. As he undressed her, slowly removing her shirt, the cool breeze over her bared breast made her breath catch.

"You smell like home to me. My home." Gerard moved her body, and when he reached between then and unbuttoned her jeans, the sound of the zipper being pulled apart soaked her pussy. "You like this. The way that I touch you. Tell me what you want, Susie. I'm yours to do with or command to do whatever you want."

"Eat me." He growled, and she could feel his cat move along his skin. "Him too. I want him to taste his mate. Then I want to let mine have you."

When he dropped to his knees, Susie felt herself sway a little. He was going to do it. And her body felt it all the way to her feet. As he pulled off her pants, leaving her panties on her, all she could think about was that he could see how wet she was, and how much she wanted to pull his mouth to her to finish her. When he slid his hands under the ties on her panties, she watched him as he tore them from her body. The climax that hit her made her want more from him. Need more of him.

He buried his mouth over her. Crying out because she wanted to feel his tongue too, Susie put her hands into his hair and held him to her, begging him to please give her what she needed. His soft laughter made her smile. Spreading her legs wide for him, as wide as she could with her pants down around her feet, Susie screamed when he opened her nether lips and blew hard over her clit.

"You're so wet." Nodding at him, begging him to take her, she looked down her body at him. "My cat wants you first. He seems to think you'll come for him."

"Yes. For you both." Gerard stood up and pulled his pants off. His shirt, already undone because he'd been working outside, was dropped at his feet as his cat took him. The big animal lunged at her, knocking her back on the bed even as she opened her thighs for him. As soon as his tongue touched her, Susie came hard and fast.

*Again, love. He wants all of you.* Her body responded to Gerard's command as if he'd pulled a string and she would follow. When she came a third and then a fourth time in the big cat's mouth, she cried out. Gerard responded by eating her ravenously.

~~~

Gerard loved the way she came for him. He ate her hungrily over and over until he knew that if he wasn't inside of her soon, he was coming all over the floor. Standing up after his cat had let him take his turn with his mate, he looked down at her body, covered in a sweet sheen of sweat that made his mouth water. There was very little about this woman that he didn't love, but watching her when she came was about the best thing he'd ever seen. Fisting his cock, he watched her watching him.

"I want to come on you like this someday. Just empty my balls all over your body and then rub it in with my body while I fuck you." Her breathless "Yes" had him sliding his hand up and down his cock faster. Her hands were all over her body...at her breasts where she pulled hard on her nipples, and at her pussy, where her fingers moved in and out of her as fast as his hand was moving up and down his cock. Holding his balls, hurting now to be empty, he nearly came all over her when she screamed out her release. But the thought of fucking her, filling her with himself, made him let his cock go in favor of sliding in and out of her.

Moving up her body, holding onto his cock, Gerard knew that as soon as he was deep into her that he was going to come. His goal now was to make her come again so that when he released, she would enjoy it as well. Taking her breast into his mouth, all of it he could, Gerard bit down and tasted her sweat with the sweet taste of her blood too. It was almost as good as her cum, but he knew there was more of her to drink from.

His cock was at her entrance when she wrapped her feet around his legs. He moved his crown in and out of her. She was so wet that he never hesitated to tease her now. When she rose up from the bed, her body taking him deeper as she cried out, Gerard filled her, buried himself to the root of his body.

He came hard, his cock moving in and out of her quicker now. And when she wrapped her legs around his waist, he pounded her again and again, taking her over the edge twice more before he leaned to her throat and licked the pulse there.

"Mark me. Mark us both." Gerard felt his teeth shift, move so that his sharper teeth were there. He bit into her, tore into her tender flesh, as his body emptied once again inside of her.

Stars danced behind his eyelids. His body, bowed back in release, felt stronger. When he felt his cat move along his skin, he worried that he was going to take him. But he only moved there, showing him that he approved of her, his mate too. When Gerard fell forward, no longer able to stay upright, he landed on the bed to the side of Susie. Pulling her up so that she lay beside him, Gerard held her while she slept, marveling that she was his now and forever.

When he woke, the room was bathed in darkness. He loved that not even the moon could reach them here, and moved his hand over the bed to touch Susie. Finding the bed not just empty but cold, he sat up, reaching for her as he did.

*I'm fine. I needed a minute.* Gerard reached for his pants to pull on when she asked him to stay where he was. *I just want to sit here, enjoy the quiet for a time. I'm not used to having so many people around all the time.*

Gerard lay back on the bed but kept his pants near. She didn't say where she was, but he had a feeling she was in the barn again. It seemed to be where she was when she wasn't working the ranch or in the house.

*I wondered if you think I could go to college.* He asked her why she didn't think she could. *Well, for one thing, it's really expensive. And another, I've never been the best student in the world. I barely made it through high school. It might be a bigger failure than high school was. I mean, I passed all my grades, but there was a great deal going on in my life then.*

*Yeah, I didn't do so well either. I did well enough, but when I think back on it, I could have been a better student. The real scholar in our family was Logan. He might have been able to go to college if it hadn't been for the ranch.* Gerard thought of Susie going to school and her being a vet. *You should do it. You'd be a wonderful vet with your little extra.*

He felt her laughter and smiled larger. *I never said I wanted to be a vet. I love animals, all of them, but I don't want to have to be around when they're sick or dying. I want to be with them when they're full of life. Playing in the sunshine and doing what they do best, just being free. I want to be an accountant.* He sat up in bed, very confused. *Don't get me wrong. If I have to be, I'll be there with one of our animals until they take their last breath. But I don't think I could handle being with the sick day after day like that. No. I want to be someone who can work with the books so that the doctor can afford to work on the animals for me. I really enjoy the neatness of the numbers. How they add up and make sense. Not like people do.*

*Okay. But again, why can't you? I mean, we could get grants. And if we needed to, I'm sure that one of my sisters-in-*

*law would give as a little loan to help you through. We'd pay them back, but…yeah, you'd be great at it.*

*I'm going to look into it. And why don't you come out here now? I'm not in the barn, but near the river that runs behind the house. Did you know that if you sit very quietly, the deer will practically come up to you and sit on your lap?*

He went to the back door and opened it to the cold night. Letting his cat take him, he thought of all the things he might do to her cat once he found her.

It took him a few minutes to find her. It wasn't that she was hiding, but he kept getting distracted by the simple beauty of the night. The pale moon would highlight something as lovely as a frostbitten branch. A small mouse getting in the last of the food before it was all covered in snow. He even paused to watch her, his Susie, as she sat on the side of the river.

She was, simply put, the most beautiful creature in all of the woods. In all of the world, he thought. Her hair was short, yet still feminine. He supposed it was to keep it out of her face, but it suited her. He had no idea what she was wearing, but it was light in color and made the darkness around her seem that much darker in comparison. As she leaned back on her hands, he could see the outline of her body, her breasts and legs, and knew that if he went to her now, she'd turn to him and smile. Gerard was thinking just how lucky he was that she'd found him when she turned and looked at him.

"You startled me." He moved toward her, taking his time, memorizing every part of her. "I was just thinking of how much I love the quiet here. The way the water running in front of me makes me think that is what an opera must sound like."

*We should go sometime. I mean, there are two opera houses not far from here, and I know that Emma has seats to them.*

*Maybe she'd let us use them once. It would be a lot of fun for us, and we could even go to a hotel afterwards and have some more fun.* He sat beside her, and his cat purred when she rubbed her hands down his back. Touching was something that he loved, his cat as well, but to be touched by her was something special. For them both. *My cat is in love with you. As much as I am.*

"I love you both as well. More than I ever thought I could a man and his beast." He lay down, resting his head on her lap and closing his eyes as she continued talking to him. "When I was in prison, the other inmates left me to myself. I guess most of them knew what I was, but it never came up in conversation. Anyway, I would spend hours and hours just being alone. Most of the time I would go to the library if I had a pass to use. Then if not, I found this broken music player with headphones. I would put them in my ears and make my own sounds. Music, I guess you could say, but with the sounds of the night. The ones you might hear if you were deep in the deepest forest with not another soul around for hundreds of miles. It started out as a way to keep people from trying to have a conversation with me. I didn't...I guess I've said this before, but I don't care for people very much. Anyway, they left me alone, and I did them as well."

*You like music then? I mean, bands and things? And so you know, I consider an opera a band.* He tried not to think of what she might have had to endure while locked away. Her cat not able to come out and run. He wondered if that was why she seemed to have such control over her. The ability to hold her when she clearly needed her. *I don't get to listen to it often. I had a player too, but a cow stepped on it when I dropped it and I never had the funds to replace it.*

"You should get you one. I guess if we start selling off the horses, we might have a little extra." They'd not talked about the money that they might have. He supposed it was easier to not think about how much it was than to get his hopes up to find out that it was all a dream. "The guy from Kentucky is coming in the morning. I guess in a couple of hours. He's coming with a lawyer too. Do you suppose he'll be fair?"

*Ed will be here, as well as the new guy that has joined the leap. He's going to be helping the family and businesses with Ed. So they'll watch out for our best interests. I just hope we can sell enough to get some money in the bank for a change. And Mason. Mason said he just wants to be here to pick my ass up when he offers me the money to buy the farm.* Gerard smiled. *He has it in his head that the guy is going to pay top dollar and hire us to breed him some winners. Sometimes I think he enjoys making fun of me. I guess because I'm the baby.*

"He loves you. As do all your brothers. And I would love to train a few of the ponies. Horses are amazing creatures, don't you think? Not the winner part, but just to breed them. Your brothers have the cattle department all sewn up. And I've never seen anyone that can make a dollar into ten like Mr. Snow can. I guess Mr. McBride, Mason's father-in-law, is like that too." He knew that about both men and was envious of them both. "Emma said that she wants to take me shopping for some clothes. I told her it would have to wait for a little while."

*I almost forgot to tell you. We have a bank account. I had no idea that we were getting paid to watch the house. I mean, Ed told me that we're being paid a rent, kind of, to stay in the house. The RA set it up for us. And Mason said that he was going to pay you too, for helping him with the animals.* She told him that she didn't need money for that. *Yeah, I told him you'd probably say that, but he said it was going to be put in the bank too. I have no idea how much, but he said that we'd have to go there in the morning…I guess today…to sign the cards to finish opening the account. Then I thought after they all leave us, we'd go and finish up getting those other clothes for you, and me some boots.*

They sat there until the sun came up and the moon moved down behind the trees. As the woods around them began to wake too, they stood up and made their way to the house. He remained his cat, not even disappointed that he'd not gotten to run her down and play, but relishing in the fact that it had been comfortable with her. Like they had known each other for decades rather than the short time they had. As they entered the house the way he'd come out, Gerard took back his body and dressed, then went to make breakfast while she cleaned up their room. Life, he decided, was about perfect.

The man sitting at his table startled him. But before he could reach out to his brother to tell him what was going on, someone put something to the back of his head. He could smell the silver even as he moved to do as he was told.

"Call out to anyone and I will have him end your life." Gerard thought of Susie just down the hall and told her to go and get Mason. She said she would go now, and he told her not to come to the kitchen. The man seemed to know what he was thinking as he continued with his threat. "If anyone comes through that door, he will blow your fucking head off before you can say anything."

"Who are you?" The gun now struck his head. "Whatever you want, you can have. But leave my wife alone."

"Why, that's what I want. And she's not your fucking wife. She's my kid, and she can have a mate only when I say she can. But she ain't gonna, not so long as I'm alive."

Gerard would gladly have ended it for him, but he wasn't sure he could take both men. "Call her in here and I swear to all that is fucking holy if she comes in here as her cat, I'm going to kill you both. Tell her that you want her to get her fucking ass in here now or you're a dead man. Might be anyway, the way I'm feeling."

"She's not here. She's meeting my sisters to go shopping." The gun hit him again, and this time the pain made him sick to his stomach. He reached up to hold onto his head and felt the blood, warm and sticky, run down the back of his neck. The next time he was hit, Gerard felt the darkness simply swallow him up.

# CHAPTER 8

Susie went out the bedroom door and let her cat take her. As she reached for Mason and the others, she told them what she knew, which really wasn't all that much. Gerard was in the kitchen, and she was sure that her father had him.

*Where are you now?* Mason sounded calm, but she'd bet anything that he wasn't. *Susie, don't go back in the house. If you get hurt, Gerard will never forgive me. We're going to come to you, but don't you dare make me have to explain to him how I let you get hurt.*

That gave her pause. *Why would he blame you if I went into the house? And if I got hurt, whose fault do you think that would be? Mine, not yours. It's not like you're here. How the hell would it be your fault?*

*Because.* She waited for more of an answer, but apparently that was all she was getting. *Just do as I said and stay back and wait for us.*

*Oh, so you think that because you're a man that I'm just not able to take care of my mate?* He started to speak, but she was already pissed off and he hadn't helped the matter. *Is that it, or is it because you're Mason Douglas? The god of all gods when it comes to cougars? Is that what you're telling me?*

*No, I'm not saying that. But you don't know if it's your father, or if he's alone. For all you know, there could be ten —* When he stopped talking, she waited. The pain in her body, the lack of connection to Gerard, made her cat whimper. *He's been hurt.*

*No shit, moron.* Susie could see into the house, but not the kitchen. Just as she was reaching for the door with her mouth—because she didn't know any other way to open it as her cat—she saw her father and a man she'd never seen before. *It's the fucking bastard, and he is with someone I don't know. They're carrying Gerard into the living room and are dumping him on the couch. He's out, but I can hear his heart...it's going strong. I swear to you, I'm going to tear his fucking ass up. Ernie's, not Gerard's. And I wanted some French toast, too.* She was babbling and she tried to stop. Never in her life had she done that, and she had no idea why she was doing it now. Nerves, she supposed, or the thought that they had her mate.

*Can you get into the house?* She wanted to ask him if it was all right now, but she was terrified beyond being even sort of nice to him, so kept her mouth shut. *You have the best bet of saving him now. I'm sorry about before. My brothers and I are about a mile from the house. We'll surround the house as soon as we get there. There is pack there too. I don't know how many, but they're rounding up now.*

*I can get in, but he'll see me. The back door is open to our bedroom. There is a double door that opens onto the deck back there. You can get in that way.* He said he could see it now. *Just don't...I'm not sure if there is anyone else in the kitchen, and I can't get in that way. I'm going to go in through the front door.* Letting her body shift just enough to open the door, Susie let it move open on its own, then went back to her cat. She felt rather than heard the wolf that seemed to appear beside her. *Paddy is here. And it looks like about a dozen of his pack. I'm going to have to make a connection to him soon, I think.*

*That would be a good idea, if I don't kill him first. He's been watching the ranch. I don't know how they got by him, but we'll talk when I see him.* Susie would not want to be Paddy when that conversation went down. When the big wolf nodded at her, she moved into the house and to the big man with the gun.

The gun went off twice, and she knew that she'd been hit as she leapt at the man. He was a bear, the one that she'd smelled on her father a few days ago. As he let his animal take him, then her, she knew that he was going to hurt her. Not only was he bigger, but he had some pretty strong drugs in his body that she could almost taste. Taking him to the floor, she heard furniture break and felt some of the splinters of wood cut into her cat. It was either keep at him or let him tear her throat out. She fought like her very life depended on it.

He tore into her skin. The scent of blood, his and hers, made her dizzy and her cat wanting more. The bear raked his great claws across her belly. She knew that she was finished when her strength felt as if it had been sucked out of her. Not willing to give up now, she started to leap at the bear again. But then she was knocked back, and five big cougars jumped on the bear, taking him down. He was dead in seconds, his body torn to pieces by the big cats. Mason went to her and stood over her as she got her breath back.

She looked at her father, and wasn't surprised to see him as his cat cornered by the wolf pack. Her body hurt. It hurt in more places than she was sure there were names for. But her cat was pleased with the outcome. Even though she'd not killed the shifter, she'd been able to hold her own until reinforcements got there to help.

Mason was standing next to her as she lay there. She would heal once she was able to shift, but she was afraid to leave, fearful of what her father might do. But Mason told her he had it and for her to go and change. Then he looked at her. She could see the look of pleading in his eyes, as if to say "For once will you do as I say?"

Christ, he was huge. So was Gerard, but Mason's cat was at least fifty pounds heavier and it was all muscle. She knew it was because he was the leap leader, but she also thought it was more than that.

His fur was covered in blood. It dripped from his muzzle and the fur around his face. She wanted to ask him if he'd been hurt, but he told her again to go and shift. That they would wait on her.

Her body ached now that she'd had time for the pain to settle in. But limping back to the bedroom to shift and pull on some clothing, she knew that she was undoubtedly the luckiest woman alive. Had they not shown up when they had, the bear would have killed her, then Gerard.

Susie looked up at him when he entered the room. He had blood on his face as well his shirt, but he looked good enough to eat up right now.

"Mason said you'd been hurt." She let her cat go and stood in front of Gerard. He pulled her into his arms and held her tightly. "You're all right then? He didn't hurt you too much? All I could think about was getting you to safety. Then I realized that you could save both of us by getting out. I have never been so afraid in all of my life."

"No. Yes. I know what you mean. Christ, if your brothers hadn't come when they had, I'd be dead. I think we both would have been. And Mason? He's fucking huge, isn't he?" Gerard held her as she cried. She wrapped her arms around him and just felt his love pour over her. "I was stupid for thinking I could take them. But to be honest, I had no idea he was the bear."

"I love you so much, Susie. You saved us by keeping a calm head. But Mason said for us to hurry. He wants this finished before things get out of hand and someone else comes to see us." The buyers. Susie nodded and started to pull away. "Not yet. I need to hold you just a couple of more minutes. He'll just have to wait."

She let him. Being held by him felt better than anything she'd ever felt. And then he finally let her go, kissing her hungrily on the mouth, and she stood there as he sat down on the bed.

"Hurry, please, or we're not leaving here." She nodded and pulled on her pants and a sweatshirt of his. When she was as dressed as she could be under the circumstances, he took her hand and they went to the living room. Her dad was still his cat, and the wolves were surrounding him. Mason, as his cat, was staring at him, with his brothers nearby. Susie thought that if she had to be on a side during a fight, she would want to be on Mason's. The man just exuded power.

"Father, just what did you hope to gain by coming here and hurting my family?"

He screamed at her that he was her family, and Gerard touched her arm as she looked at him.

*Tell him to shift. Tell him to shift…be specific or you'll pull them all. We can't understand him, and if he's human, or at least looks human, we can hear him spew his bullshit.* She told him that she couldn't, she wasn't a leader. *Trust me, love, you can do it. And when you do, he's going to know real power when he sees it. He has no idea that you're more powerful than him, and when he figures it out, I'm glad to be here to see his face. The man is going to know who the real boss is of his little world before he dies.*

Not at all sure what he meant, she turned back to her father. His cat was old, graying around the muzzle, and he'd gained weight. She wondered briefly if he could even get up and run much, and then thought about what Gerard had told her. She looked at Mason. After giving her a short nod, he lay down on the floor as if he had nothing in the world to be worried about. Susie looked at her father.

"Ernest Benjamin, shift."

Had she not been there, or even heard that it could be done, she wasn't sure she would have believed it possible. But he did shift, and not only that, from the sound of it, it hurt him badly. She wanted to dance and clap her hands, but instead she just stared at him like this was something she did every day. He stared at her as if he wanted her dead, which, under the circumstances, he more than likely did.

"You fucking cunt. Why the hell did you have them do that to me? Christ, that fucking hurt. You don't know what you've done now, do you? You've pissed me off is what you did. And now I'm gonna teach you a lesson you won't ever forget." He started to stand and realized he was naked. "Give me something to put on, for fuck sake. I'm not gonna address this leap with my bare ass showing. And when I'm done, you and I are gonna talk."

He laughed. The same laugh she'd heard all her life when he was standing over her, beating her with his belt or anything else that he could reach. Raising her chin, she addressed him in a way that made her cat purr along her skin in approval.

"Then you should have thought of that before you came barging into my life. And they didn't do this to you. I did it. I'm stronger than you are." When he lunged at her, she laughed when he fell on the floor. As he got back up and started to come at her, Mason stood up and growled low. "I'd heed him if I were you. You're in enough trouble as it is. Did you know that you're to report to him when you're in his area? And when you're here, you're to abide by his laws? You never told me that. Never let on like there were laws that had to be followed by our kind. Not to mention, some of the shit you told me wasn't even right. You lied to me my whole life. And you know what, Ernie? I sort of like the way Mason follows the laws. It's com—"

"Fuck his laws. I came here to get you, and by God, I'm getting you. Now get me some fucking clothes. I'm not gonna tell you again. I'm your father, goddammit." She thought about what he'd said, and it occurred to her that he was nothing to her. Nothing but the donor to her mother's egg. "Susan Benjamin, you are trying me right now. And you know what happens when I get myself in a state. You ain't gonna have no one to blame for your pain but your own mouth. Get me something to put on."

"No." He just stared at her. "No, I'm not going to do a thing for you. I'm not going to help you, and I'm certainly not going to save you should this man want you dead. And it's not Benjamin, you flabby piece of shit. It's Douglas now. I'm Susan Douglas."

*Oh, he's dead all right. I'm just wanting you to have your final words to him.* Susie looked at Mason when he spoke to her. *He killed one of my men to get here. He also killed three wolves that were guarding this land. He and the bear broke the law. Not just pack or my law, but the human law too. He has to die.*

"Mason said that you might as well tell me everything on your mind. I'm thinking that won't take too terribly long, as small minded as you are. Because when you're taken from my house, they're going to show you what it means to fuck with someone bigger than you." Her father started cursing again, and she only smiled. "I really do hate you. I never realized I did until this very moment. I haven't ever had any respect for you or Mother, but you did bring me into this world, so I thought that I could at least try. But it was a waste of my energy and my time. You made sure of that the moment you took off your belt that first time we met and beat me with it. Then stood over me and laughed when I begged you to please love me."

"You think we wanted you? Hell no. And the fact that she didn't tell me until it was too late to knock you out of her is the only reason you're here. 'Course, being in prison like I was helped you to be born, but had I been out, you wouldn't even have been nothing but a stain on the floor when I was done with her. But you served some purpose. And you will again. These here men? They got no reason to murder me. And that's what it would be, murder. I was just doing what I needed to do to bring you to heel." He stood up then, and she could see that the years hadn't been good to him. "I'm going to kill this pack of babies. Then I'm going to come in here and beat you to shit. Then when you're dying, I'm going to take that man you call your mate, and I'm going to cut his throat and let you watch him bleed all over the floor. You think you can just end my life like I was nothing? You're fucked up if you think that's gonna happen. I am your father, no matter how much you might hate that fact."

"Kill him." The wolves moved as one, but it was the leap that took her father to the floor. They were playing with him, she thought, until she realized they were running him out of the house. Because the moment he was out in the yard, they all pounced on him as one, and his screams were cut off almost as soon as they started.

She looked at Gerard. He didn't say a word, but pulled her to him and kissed her. Tears, she knew, were flowing down her face, and all she could think of was that she'd just murdered a man. Not just any man, but her father. Looking around the ruined room, she leaned on Gerard as he held her.

The body of a naked man was just behind her. She could see his feet as well as the blood that had pooled beneath his body. The coffee table, even though it was old, was shattered, as was the only lamp they had in the room, and the television had a large splinter of wood sticking out of the center of it. Framed pictures were broken; photos of people she didn't know were ruined as well. And the cushions on the couch were stained dark. Going down the hall to the bedroom, she made her way out to the deck that looked out over the woods and sat on the only chair out there. Gerard joined her, but only leaned against what was left of the railing that the Mitchells had never fixed.

"We don't have to stay here." She thought about it and shook her head. "You and I can...I don't know. Live with my aunt until something comes along we can afford. Or we can rent an apartment. It'll be tough going for a little while, but we can do it."

"I think we should live here. And buy it if they'll sell it to us at a reasonable price." He nodded and grinned. "This place has seen a lot of horrible things. I'd like to fill it with good memories. Our memories. Children, too, if you want. I do want them. I'm not sure what kind of mother I'd make, but I think I could do all right with you and your family's help."

"There's a dead man on the front lawn and one in the living room. I don't think we can go anywhere but up, honey." He was joking, but it still made her shiver. "I'm sorry. That was callus of me. But I would love to have children with you. Lots of them. Running around our feet and then taking care of us when we're too old to get around very much. I love you."

"No, you weren't callus. It was honest, and right now I need that. And I love you more than simple words could say." He just watched her, and it comforted her somewhat that he didn't feel the need to fill in the silence. She thought of the man that now lay dead in their yard. She refused to think of him as her father. He was nothing more than a person that had been a thorn in her side for as long as she could remember. "He didn't love me. Not even to find that I was his child and a part of him. And I know that my mother felt even less for me, if that's possible."

"They brought you into this world, and for that alone I will be grateful to them. Without you, I'd be nothing. Less than nothing." Susie felt the tears threaten again. "I want us to have some children soon. I know that things are tight right now, but we can make it. My aunt raised us six boys on nothing more than a shoestring and some bubblegum."

"I'd like that very much." She could hear things in the house now. Furniture being moved. They were removing the bear/man, and she was happy that they'd not have to deal with that. It was too much to think of right now, so she tried to think of anything else. "I want to talk to Emma and Holly. They both said that they'd help me get started on a few things. I'll need startup capital to get the horses trained to be sold."

126

"All right." She looked at him, and he knelt down in front of her and took her hand. "I love you. And if we can make a little money off the sale, we'll get us some much needed things for the house. I think our couch and television are shot. Not to mention our only lamp is now broken glass and electrical parts." They both laughed, and she kissed his hand that held hers.

"I love you, Gerard." He kissed her hand and told her that he loved her too. "I guess we'd better go see to this. That guy will be here at ten. And I don't know about you, but I'd rather there wasn't blood and gore in the house when he comes by. Might make him not what to buy a horse from us."

Going into the living room, they both stood still and looked around. In the little time they'd been gone, things had not just been picked up, but all the furniture, including the rugs, had been removed from the room. They went outside just as the couch was being loaded in the huge dumpster that had been brought to clean the barns. Mason came toward them just as a delivery truck was pulling in. She just knew that the family had been busy for them.

"You're going to be pissed off. So if you want to hurt someone, then you should hurt Zack. He can take it." The man in question laughed but didn't offer himself up for sacrifice. "Also, you should know that I'm sorry. I shouldn't have assumed anything with you. I won't make that mistake again."

"I'm sorry as well. I was scared. And worried. I was out of line to talk to you that way." Mason put out his hand. "You aren't off the hook for whatever is in that truck. We'll pay you back for it if it takes us all our lives."

"Deal. But I don't think you're going to have to wait that long to pay me. I'm pretty sure you're going to make enough today to settle up right away." She only nodded. "Trust me."

She laughed and so did he. Things around here were never going to be calm, she thought. And really? She didn't think she wanted it to be.

~~~

Gerard had never been around someone who knew horses as well as the three men that had shown up at nine-thirty. The big man, Carl Jackson, was the money man and good-old-boy in a loud and boisterous way. His trainer, Steve Glenn, didn't say much, but Gerard was pretty sure he saw everything. And he watched Susie like she was going to give him divine powers. Then there was the lawyer, Paul Garrison.

There was something profoundly calming about him. He was a shifter, he knew that, but what kind he'd not figured out as yet. Every time he thought he had a handle on it, he'd move in a way that made him realize that was wrong. Gerard looked at the house when he heard someone cursing. It was Zach, and if he was right, his aunt was going to tear him a new butt for doing it, as she was standing right next to him when he started. Even from where he was, Gerard knew that he'd smashed his thumb with the hammer and he was trying not to curse any more as Aunt Georgie stood near him tapping her foot.

If he was honest with himself, he was glad for the help on the house. The cleaning crew, a bunch of women from the wolf pack, had come in to give the house a good cleaning. They'd moved in while the stuff was still covered and most of it was still under sheets, and neither he nor Susie had spent a great deal of time in the house other than to sleep or eat. But the stain in the living room and the broken stuff had made it difficult to ignore any longer. And the furniture was something altogether different.

The truck that had come in was full of everything. Couch, love seat, as well as several lamps that seemed to light up all the corners and make the room look cheery. The stain on the floor had been removed. He'd not asked how, but was glad that it was no longer there. Even the bedroom furniture had been a wonderful addition. There was a larger bed for their room, as well as two dressers and a couple dozen packages of hangers, something they'd not had at all.

New towels were being washed, as well as curtains hung at all the now clean windows. Someone had even thought to get them a new fancy grill that did everything but eat the food for them, it seemed, as well as patio furniture. Zach and Logan were working on the new railing, as the old was just too bad to save. Their house was beginning to take on the shape of something they could be proud of. And he'd be paying his brother back for decades, he thought. He looked at Carl when he laughed, making him aware that he should have been paying attention.

"Well there, young man, what do you think if I do that?" He felt his face heat up when he realized he'd not a clue what he was talking about. When he laughed, Gerard knew that he understood. "I want to buy two dozen now, and the little lady there is going to train me a dozen more. My trainer is gonna tell her what we need, but I don't think she's gonna need much in the way of help on that score. That's a right smart wife you have there."

"She is at that." He wanted to go to her and hold her, but she was talking to Steve again. Ed had shown up about ten, and since it was going on eleven-thirty now, he wondered what the next buyer would say when he got there. Gerard was hoping for enough money to put down on the house.

"You love her, don't you? I mean, you really do and truly love that girl." Gerard said that he did. "Never seen a man so much in love with his wife before. Suppose it could be the cougar thing. My man over there, Paul, he's one of them elites."

"I wondered." Gerard told him that he'd have to talk to his attorney about the sale. "I don't know a great deal about it, but Ed does. He's sharp as any lawyer I've ever met. And an honest one. You won't have to worry about him cheating you." Carl said he wasn't worried on that score one bit.

As they made their way to the house, he wondered what sort of mess there was in there, and was surprised to find not just the new stuff set up, but the entire house was spotless and the women were putting together some lunch. His aunt came into the kitchen and asked Carl if he and his men would join them for lunch. The ladies had things about done.

"Sure thing. We was gonna go and have us a steak lunch at the diner, but they don't have that on their menu. I'm a meat and potato sort of man. I guess you guys are too." Aunt Georgie told him that they had both on their menu today. "Well, that's mighty nice of you. Now, we'll get these here kids all tidied up, and then be able to enjoy some good food."

Gerard made his way back out to the horses and Susie when Carl, Ed, and Paul shut themselves up in the office. He wondered if there was any furniture in there, but decided that they'd make do. He thought there might have been a desk in there and maybe his laptop, but he'd been so busy lately that he'd not used it in a while.

Susie was in the barn with Mason and Darin when he got to the fence. He entered just as the shouting was starting.

"I don't care what you think you have to do, I said no." Mason growled at Susie, and Gerard decided that he'd stand back; she seemed to have this one. "You take it back right now. If you don't, then I'll...I'll tell Emma on you."

"It was Emma's idea." That shut her up, and she turned to glare at him. Mason laughed as he continued. "Don't take it out on him, either. He had no idea what we were doing."

"They're giving us the house and the land. Actually, they already did it. It's been in our name for three days now." Gerard looked at Mason, who nodded. "And get this...they think that whatever we make from the sale of the horses goes into our account, and they don't want any of it. That's not right."

Darin cleared his throat before speaking. "While I don't want to be blasted by her—damn, but you have a fine temper—I think it's a good arrangement. Selling the horses is going to help us in ways that you can't see right now. The men who come here are gonna need a place to stay, places to eat, as well as someone to cart their butts around town. It's going to give our town the boost it needs. And giving you the house and land? It's only what you should have had at the first. You're making this ranch viable again. And it needed it for a lot longer than since you two came here. You should consider building a B&B to work with too. Maybe here on the land so that they're close when the deal is done."

Gerard thought it was really stretching it. And it would be costly too. But right now he had to help Susie, and he didn't want her pissed at him. The idea to help the town out did have its merits.

He told her what he thought. "While I know that most of that is out of our reach for the moment, I can see where it would help the town. It's dying. A lot of the buildings downtown are for sale. Most of them are boarded up, and those that aren't are going to need some major work on them to get them up and sellable. Maybe we should at least look at this from that standpoint."

Susie huffed, but he could tell that she liked the idea. Perhaps it was that it came from Mason that really had her pissy. He loved the way she worked things out in her head before speaking. But when she looked at Mason, he knew it was going to be great, whatever she said to him.

"Do you always get your way?" Susie glared at Mason when all he did was grin at her. "I really dislike you right now. And if you know what's good for you, you'll leave me alone while I think of a way to get back at you."

"Yes, ma'am." As he walked by her, he winked at Gerard, then tipped back his hat and smiled. "Miss Susie, I do believe that I like you. Very much. You're a handful, a pain in the ass, and you give as good as you get, but I like that about you. I'm very glad that you're my family and not my enemy. I'd hate to think how you'd try to hurt me."

"You might want to keep looking over your shoulder for a while then." He laughed and moved out of the barn. Darin stayed behind and just shook his head.

"I'll run it." They both looked at him. "The B&B. I really want to do it. I've been thinking of branching out and…well, to be honest, I haven't wanted to be a rancher for a while. I might grow to hate it if I hang around much longer. I'll even cut you a deal on running the place for you." Susie asked him why he thought it would work.

"Because I know how much they're paying you for the horses. And I know that so long as you want, the horses will come to you and you'll make them a better place. I don't know how I know that, but I do. And not just here, but with other men and women in town as well. I was being honest when I told you what you and my other brothers' ranches are going to do for this little town. We're going to be a tourist trap, sure, but the people will be making money and that's what is important."

"I don't know anything about running a ranch this size." Darin said he knew less about running a B&B. "So why do you think you can do it?"

"Because, little brother, we're family, and we'll work it until it does work." He moved out of the barn then and also tipped his hat at Susie. He was whistling as he made his way out into the sunshine, and Gerard looked at Susie.

"What do you think?" She told him she had no idea. "Me neither. That other guy, do you suppose he'll buy some horses too? Make you another offer like Carl did?"

"I don't know that either." He grinned at her. "What does that mean? You think this is funny?"

"No. I think it's wonderful. Come on, my lady wife, let's go and see if we can make some very rich men happy. And if we make a few bucks on the deal, I'm all the happier for it." He kissed the back of her hand when he took it. "And maybe if you're really good today, I'll let you tie me to the bed later and have your way with me. We have to break it in, don't we? Oh, and so you know, the house looks great. I think we can make that part work too."

"I hope so." But he noticed that she no longer seemed to be unhappy. "Gerard, do you really think we can make the town better by putting in a B&B? I mean, I don't know about the other stuff, but that sounds kind of fun. I've never been in one before, but I've seen them. And Darin can do it if he wants."

He thought that of all his brothers, Darin would be the one to make it work. He was the friendliest person he knew and could talk to anyone. As they worked around the corral, taking notes on what had to be done to the barns and fencing, Gerard felt better about things than he had in a very long time.

# CHAPTER 9

"Did you get in?" Howard told him that he hadn't, but he was working on it. "What does that mean, you're working on it? You should have been in and out of the place weeks ago. I need you to burn that shit to the ground."

"They got themselves some vid-e-o cameras all over the place, and if that ain't enough, there are any number of men just moving around the building like they got nothing better to do than to keep me off the land. Why you suppose they went and done that, Garth? That ain't right." Garth stood up, and Howard could see that he was pissed too. But he also knew that he'd be over it in five minutes, as he wouldn't remember what it was about. Garth also wanted to tell his brother that the word *video* was just one word, not three, but didn't. If he corrected him every time he screwed up, they'd never have a conversation. "I got just as much banking in me getting in that place as you do. If they find that stash of ours, we're as good as broke. Might as well turn our hiney's in on how much we got to run on right now, right? I mean, I only gots twelve dollars now that I had to get me some burny stuff. That girl that knocked me down, she let me get me all fired up. That wasn't really

135

very nice of her either, I'm thinking. She has to pay me back for that, don't you think, Garth?"

Garth didn't mention to him that there wasn't enough for him and Howard to run on anyway. He'd been double dipping on the cash long before the town began to show signs of being taken over by the fucking Douglases. Then there were the Snows and McBrides. Those people were making his life a living hell right now. Instead of the fifty million that they'd been putting in the safe under the building, there was more like ten million. Just enough for him to get out of the country. He had no idea what to do about his brother other than to have him locked up again, but that was going to be hard on his little brother. Howard hated that place.

Twenty-two years ago Garth had begun the plan to take the town. It wasn't as grand as it could have been, but since the place butted up against some of the prettiest hills he'd ever seen and the river ran right though some of the nicest land that there was, he thought about making himself some money. There would be several hotels, of course, but his plan had been to put in some of them little houses and rent them out to stupid city folks. Ones that would pay him a great deal of money to get away. From what, he wasn't so sure, but he'd rake in the cash. His brother hadn't been a part of the plan then, and he wasn't in it all that much now that he had to run with his tail between his legs.

Then the banker, Nigel Rogers, had come up with the plan to run some of the people out. Just make their lives too hard to hang around, and they'd collect on their misfortune by taking their land and anything else that they might have. Money was the big thing. Rogers, the stupidest person he'd ever met other than Howard, could foreclose on the land and that was what they needed. Of course they'd had to bring some heavy hitters too. The kind that would do whatever they told them for the right price. It had been the best money ever spent as far as he was concerned. Then the Snow bitch had started sniffing around. But the little prick Rogers had had his own agenda, and had fucked them all over by not just getting caught, but also bringing in the Feds.

"That money, do you have any idea what kind of stuff we can do with that when we get out of the state? I'm gonna get me a whole bunch of matches. Those kind that are sticks, not the paper kind. They don't burn good like I want. Them people, they can't do nothing to us if we just move out. Whatcha think, Garth? We can just go to someplace else and never come back here. I might. Just to see if I can burn that house down. But not the barn. It's got some pretty horses in it, and I don't wanna hurt them." He wanted to correct his brother again but didn't. It only served to piss him off when he did, and he would never learn anyway. "I'm thinking with my half, I'm going to buy me a little island and have them naked women waiting on me hand over my feet."

"Hand over foot, you moron, and that isn't going to work at all if you don't get in and get the fucking money anyway. I'd do it, but my face is known and I'm going to get killed or lynched if I so much as go in the place." Howard nodded and started to pace his room.

Garth had been staying in this place for three months now. And he was sick to death of it. There were no women that he could call on to come and help a man out. The restaurants that he would love to try were places that took more cash than he had, and his credit cards were no good any more. He couldn't even get him a nice fake one, not without any money. He was broke, seriously broke, with only about a grand on his person. Not enough to get far when you were a wanted man. He should have been better prepared when Rogers went down. Lighting a cigarette, he thought about the fucking idiot.

Rogers getting caught had been both a blessing and a pain in the ass. The man had been acting all loony for a few months by then, and Garth had a feeling that he was making his own little escape plan. Then he up and disappeared, and Garth had a feeling that the Douglases knew about that too. But they'd all thought they were free and clear, until that fucking family had to go and stick their nose in his business.

"You thinking what I'm thinking?" Garth hoped the fuck not. Howard was his only brother and sometimes he wished he'd never met the man. He was as stupid as they came. "I'm thinking when they do that grand opening thing next time at the mill, we should go and get some of the giveaway things they're gonna have. Stick it to them."

"Yes, that'll make such an impression on them for us to take some dollar items that aren't worth the plastic it was printed on." Howard nodded and Garth felt like finding something to kill him with. "We'll have to get the money before the grand opening. They're going to have that place open twenty-four seven for a while, and there won't be any time to get in."

"We just need to go in when they're closed is all. Which twenty-four do you suppose they're gonna be open? And if they're only open seven days, we can go in after that. I'm thinking that we can make a killing on taking some of the stock too. They sure have a lot for someone that's only going to be—"

"Shut up." He rubbed his temples again, thinking that he might have worn a place in his skull by now. "We have to get in before they open up. And that's in two days. Less if they have any more stock coming in and people have to go in and set it up again. Did you see about getting in on that? Being one of the stock boys."

"Said that I'd not work out on account of I can't read. I thought it'd be 'cause of my face and hands, but they never even said a word about it." He sat down and huffed. "Don't know what they need me to read for them. All I gotta do is match the stuff up to the stuff already on the shelf. Seems even a fool could do that."

"If you're stocking the shelves, moron, then there won't be anything there for you to match up, now will there?" Howard started to speak but then looked as if he got it. "Yes. Pictures don't work if you don't have anything to match it to."

"You know, that's just not right. They should have special jobs for people who got no ability to read signs." He wanted to tell him that they did have special jobs for people like him, but didn't. Howard was, after all, his only brother, much to his dismay. "You think I can get me a job working in one of them fancy shops that are opening?"

"Doing what? I'm pretty sure when you ever get around to getting our money out and then burning the mill down, no one is going to want you to work for them. And to work in a fancy shop, you have to still be able to read." Howard smiled when he mentioned burning the place down. "You can do that, right? Burn it to the ground?"

"That's what I can do best. And so's you know, I have that all worked out too. Got me some gasoline and some cotton. I'm figuring that the place will just puff up when it's started too. Made of wood and all, it won't be no time for it to come down on some heads." His brother had that look in his eyes as he talked about the mill burning. It was what he was good at, as he'd said, and he loved it. When they were children, Howard would sit and watch the fireplace in their home for hours, never saying a word but having a glassy look in his eyes that Garth knew meant insanity. Howard's cheese had slipped off his cracker, as his mom used to say.

When he'd been about six, Howard had decided to burn down the abandoned playhouse that had sat in their yard for years. Neither he nor Howard had ever played in the thing, but sometimes the neighborhood girls would come over and have tea parties in it or something. Howard had never made allowances for anyone being in the small house when he'd gotten into his head to play with matches.

The girls, three of them, had all died. The doors to the house had been barricaded, and there had been no way for them to get out once the lick of flames had begun to take the house over. Not only had he made sure that the structure had stayed as intact as he could make it when it started to burn, but the little girls had not been able to get out, no matter how loudly they'd screamed to be let go.

His brother had been put into a facility for the criminally insane. His mom and he had gone to see Howard once a week for a while, then less as he got older. After their mother had died, Garth went to see his brother often, but only to make sure that he continued to get his brother's check that was sent to the house to help with medical bills. He banked on that income until the money started coming in from the land deals.

Then about ten years ago, almost to the day, Howard was let out. There wasn't any reason, they said, to keep him, as he'd not done anything like that again. Of course, immediately after his release, he burned down two more buildings and set a gas station on fire, taking the lives of four people. It seemed to Garth that no one had taken into consideration that he'd not set any fire because no one had given him matches, his favorite thing to use, and a building he could play with.

And now, five years later, he was still out, and no one had bothered to see if he had anything to do with the fires that had been set around the states surrounding them. He had no idea if it was because they'd deemed him fit or they just didn't care. Whatever the reason, Howard was a murderer, pure and simple. Garth had convinced him that he'd better go out of town to have his fun and to check to see if there was anyone in the buildings before he did it. All he must have heard was go out of town to fire houses, because there had been a dozen or so deaths in the last year alone.

"I'm going to go and check the place out again. I'm thinking those cameras won't work at night, and I can get me in then." He wanted to tell him he was sure he was wrong but said nothing. He wanted some quiet time, not listening to his brother jabber about nothing.

When the room was quiet, he went to lay down on the bed. Just lately he'd been having trouble sleeping, and he wasn't sure if it was the money bothering him or just plain boredom. He was really bored, and it was mostly because he didn't have people to talk to. He didn't count Howard, because it was difficult enough to talk to him when he wasn't aggravated. But when he was upset, like he'd been since the fire at the Mitchell ranch, he was impossible to have a conversation with.

The mill had been Garth's baby. Yes, it was a great way to make money, and when he'd hit on the idea of double charging the ranches, it had been a stroke of genius on his part when most of them just paid the bill every month without a single complaint. There were a few, of course, that just let it pile up and up, but he'd taken care of that by charging them late fees and then interest that would amount to almost double what they'd thought they owed in the first place. But then that fucking Snow moved in and had some things looked into. If he'd been smart, he'd have taken his money and ran then. But he had hung out, hoping that he could pull off letting them think it was all Rogers's doing. He still remembered the conversation to this day he'd had with Palmer Snow.

"You do know that no one is going to believe that you had nothing to do with the billing that came from your office, don't you? I mean, come on, you didn't even get the names right on three of them. Michelle instead of Mitchell, and Jason instead of Jace? And my all-time favorite is McBirdy instead of McBride. What were you thinking? Or were you?" Garth had picked up the bills and looked at them. He'd gone to a lot of trouble to get them right, even using the spell checker thing on his computer. "Jason Douglas does not exist. So you'd never be able to collect on these anyway."

"Who names their kid Jace anyway?" He looked at Palmer when he didn't answer him. "You know that I had nothing to do with these bills. It's all Rogers. He's the one that holds all the deeds on the ranches. Why aren't you talking to him?"

"I did. He's in jail. I had the pleasure of watching him being arrested. Are you going to give me a good time too? He nearly pissed himself trying to convince anyone and everyone that he was innocent. Much like you are." He stood up and smiled. "You'll never get away with this. Trust me when I tell you, I'm going to take great pleasure in watching you fall too."

And since then, he'd been hiding out. Not far really...right under their noses, as a matter of fact, but hiding all the same. And now things were about to come to a head, and he couldn't get to his money to run. Mother fuck balls.

"Never happened did it, you ass hat? You never got to see me squirm like Rogers did, now did you? You and that daughter of yours, they really fucked me over, but I won anyway." Garth laid a pillow over his head to try and stop the pounding. Lately it was all he could do to make it a whole day without having a painful head. He'd go to the doctor, but he didn't have one that would see him, and even if he did, there wasn't enough money to pay him once he did.

"I'll have all I need soon. If my dumbassed brother ever gets in and out. Maybe he'll get caught and I can just not have to tell him where his money went." Closing his eyes against the pain, Garth decided that he might leave a tip on where to find his brother once he had the money. He liked that idea very much, and was smiling when he felt sleep take him under.

~~~

Susie moved around the office and tried to think what she was doing there. Emma had told her she was perfect for the job, but she had answered the phone wrong twice now, and she wasn't sure it was a good idea if she was to try a third time. When the stupid thing decided to make a noise again, she actually thought about just ignoring it, but snatched it up anyway.

"Clarke and Banner Law Office." Well, she got that part right. "How may I help you, please?"

"You sound so professional, my dear. Keep up the good work." She smiled at Mr. Snow and asked him what she could do for him. "Is Ed around? I have some information on Vance for him, and I'd like for him to check it out."

"Mr. Clarke is still talking with the men from Kentucky. He just asked me to order in some dinner for them. I'm thinking it's not going well." He asked her why. "Well, yesterday when they all left the house, I thought it was a done deal, but then today Mr. Jackson called to say he wanted to make some changes. I'm not sure what it is. And Mr. Banner is talking to the other man...Mr. Rose. I think he's still working on if he wants any or not."

"I'm sure it will be fine. And from what I've heard, you have some lovely horses out there. I was going to come out and have a look myself. Always trying to branch out. Oh, and before I forget to tell you, I have someone coming out that might want to help you out on the ranch. Her name is...let me see if I can find it in my mess here." She made notes on things that she needed to pick up at the store on the way home. Gerard said he'd cook and she had to pick up something she wanted. Lately it had been just hamburger, but he said he wanted a steak and all the trimmings. She was going to get it for them too. "Oh yes. Her name is Crosby. Mercedes Crosby. She can work with the horses or any other animal that you might have around. A vet of the highest regard. But a little...well, she's stressed out over some personal issues, and needs a place to mellow out. Can't think of any other place for her to do so."

"Mr. Snow, I don't know if we can afford to have a vet around fulltime. That's a lot to have going for us right now." He told her not to worry about it. "But I have to. If she comes here to work, she's going to expect to get paid, I'm pretty sure."

"The RA is paying her wages, and I'm to understand that until she finds her a place to buy, she's going to be staying at the local hotel. Nice woman—you and the other women are going to just love her." Susie tried to calm her temper. The RA had, as far as she could see, an endless supply of money. "And they're paying for her hotel too. Just until things are settled with your end of this."

She told him that she'd talk to Gerard and see what he had to say. Whoever this Crosby woman was, she was going to be in for a rude awakening if she thought the DD had any funds from their end. At least coming from her and Gerard's part of the ranch. Last night they'd spent over two hundred dollars on just a pair of boots. They were really good ones, but that was a lot of money for them. And then they'd gone to the grocery store.

After hanging up with Palmer—as he insisted on her calling him—she looked over the files that Mr. Banner had given her this morning when she'd gotten there. Most of it was things like insurance policies, as well as an employee benefit program. She just wanted a job, not all the stuff that went with it that would drain her check before she got it.

When his door opened, she turned to see the two men that had come in when she'd gotten there…Mr. Rose, who owned Rose Racings, and his attorney, Mr. Burks.

Both men shook hands with her and smiled a lot. And when Mr. Burks sat down on the corner of her desk, she felt her cat move along her skin like she wasn't too happy with him. He only smiled at her.

"Did you know that Mr. Rose owns the finest lanes in the country? Not just the finest, but also to be considered the fastest, as well as having the most winners coming out of his farms. They call them farms in Louisiana." She had no idea what he was talking about and said as much. "Well, my dear Mrs. Douglas, he wants you to find him a winner.

And he's willing to pay top dollar to have said winner. You are very wealthy."

"I don't understand." He stood up when Mr. Clark's door opened, and those men came out into her area as well. They had, apparently, decided to go out to dinner. She was glad now that she'd told the restaurant that she'd call them back with a time.

"You can get in touch with your husband, right?" Nodding, she asked Mr. Clark where he was needed. "Dinner. We're all going to dinner to celebrate. I'm telling you, I've never had so much fun. Why don't you tell the family to come on in? We might as well celebrate in style. And Palmer too. Tell him to get his butt in here too." The man was nearly giddy, and she found herself smiling when she reached for Gerard.

*Do you know what they came to on a price?* She said that she'd not been told, but they were celebrating. *Maybe we have enough to fix the barn roof. The thing just gave way today when we were trying to patch it up. I'm telling you, Susie, if the Mitchells were here now, I'd be hard pressed not to hit one of them. I know that he's gone and all, but he should have taken better care of his home, if nothing else, for the animals he took in.*

*I'm sorry. I wish I could do more to help out. But this job will help us out.* He said he was glad for it in the event that the horses turned out to be a bust. *I love you, but come on into town. The rest of your brothers as well. I'm to call Palmer in, as well as Aunt Georgie.*

After he told her that he'd contact the rest of the family, she picked up the phone to call Palmer. He said that he'd been talking to Ed and was on his way in. He also said that he needed to talk to her too.

"I'm hoping for good news. For you both."

So was she. There were things that they wanted to do to the house that hadn't been done by Emma and Holly. The furniture was nice, but she needed new underwear and shoes for the barn. Not necessarily in that order, but she needed them all the same. Thinking how much they might cost, she nearly missed what Palmer said.

"I'm sorry. Did you say that you have a ring for Aunt Georgie?" He laughed and said that he did. "You're going to ask her to marry you? Tonight?"

"I will if you don't think it will take away from your night. I've been wanting to do if for a while now, but she just keeps changing the subject. Tonight I'm going to get down on my knee and beg her." She told him she thought that was a wonderful idea and he should go for it. "I think I will. Yes, sir, I really think I will."

As she left the office with the men, she thought of the man she'd seen earlier hanging around the mill. It was right across the street from her job, so she had a good look at him. He looked like the man that she'd seen at the ranch, but she wasn't really sure. If she could get near him, then she'd know for sure. It had been dark and he'd been in front of her, not where she could see his face, but she had a feeling that she'd know him for some reason. As she moved out onto the street and into the awaiting car, she looked around. He was there, she was sure. But where? She wasn't positive. Just the feelings of being watched had her cat humming to be freed.

The restaurant wasn't ready for a party their size, so she stepped outside to be out of the noise. It was still something she was trying to get used to, all the people in her life now. And when she saw the man again, she turned her back to him as he moved down the street mumbling about cameras and the number twenty-four. As he passed her, she pretended to be window shopping, and when he walked by her, she took a deep breath and thought she'd made a mistake until he touched her arm.

"Hey." He jerked her around and she stared at him. Someone had burned him badly at some point in his life. His face was scarred badly, his lips were not even, like the skin had melted in the wrong way. His brow was gone over his left eye, and his nose had a smashed in look to it. It was almost grotesque, but she also felt sorry for him. "I know you. You're that woman that's been hanging around the ranch. And you pushed me in the fire. You burned my hands that night. I had to buy some medicine so it'd not get all pus-like. You owe me for that. Okay?"

"No, it's not okay. You were trying to burn down my house." He grinned at her and told her that was the plan. "Why?"

"I like the pretty colors when it goes up. Did you know that if there is other things in the house, like cotton and stuff, it'll make such pretty colors? I love to see that. But my brother said that I can't be playing around here. He'd get caught and I'd be in deep shit, he said, if there was nobody to take any care of me." She nodded, not sure what he was talking about but said nothing. "You'll have to come with me now. He said that if I seen you again, I'm to bring you to him. He'd like a word or two with you. My brother sure is mad at them Douglas guys. You know them? He said they messed things up bad for him and me."

"I don't want to go with you. I'm having dinner with my husband." He looked around and then back at her. "They're coming now. You can join us if you want. I'm sure that they'd like that. We're having steak and fries I think. And pie for dessert. You like pie, don't you?"

"I like cupcakes better. They gots them lots of icing on them. I'm hungry, that's for sure. But I and my brother have to get the money so we can go away. I'm going to buy me an island and have naked women waiting on me hand and feet…foot. He said it was hand and foot." Susie nodded and saw Gerard, Darin, and Zach coming toward her. She stopped them but told them to play along.

"There they are now. See, you guys don't mind if he joins us, do you? He's the man that was trying to burn our house down." She was careful not to say any names and warned them not to either. She didn't know why, but she was thinking he might spook if he knew they were the Douglas family. "He was telling me about his brother. I didn't catch his name." She looked at the scarred man and waited.

"My brother is Garth Vance. He used to run the mill until he was caught stealing. Now me and him are gonna get our stash and go away. It's the only way I can have me my island." Mason came out too, but he stayed back when she asked him to. She had no idea why, but she thought perhaps this man knew what he might look like. When the man with her started telling the rest about the island and the women, she reached out to Mason.

*He is the brother to Garth Vance. Why does that name sound familiar besides running the mill?* He told her. *So he's the man that tried to have you all sent out on a rail for nonpayment of bills? This guy was in on that?*

*No. Not him, but I do know who he is. I think everyone does, as a matter of fact. His name is Howard Vance. He's been in and out of mental hospitals for years. He killed a bunch of people when he was younger…young girls, I think. That's how he was burnt. I guess one of the girls in the building fell against him when she was…. Never mind. He's not right.* She told him she'd figured that already. *I don't understand. What's he doing here now?*

*He's the man that tried to set fire to the house that night. And he was telling me about a stash in the mill.* He took a step toward them. *Mason, if you spook him now, we'll never find out where his brother is, and I'm pretty sure a lot of people want to know that.*

*He's wanted by the FBI as well as state and local police. I'm pretty sure that...this stash, did he say how much was in it? From what I've heard from Palmer, there are millions missing. Not just in money he got from ranchers, but from insurance fraud, double billing of companies he dealt with, and a number of other things.* She told him that all he'd said was that he was going to buy an island. *So they're planning to scat. If you had asked me, I would have thought that he'd already left town. But if he's waiting to collect on some money, that could explain it.*

*That's what I'm assuming. And you should also know that he has no remorse about trying to burn down the house. It's as if he has no idea that it's wrong. And his brother, do you suppose he encourages him to do this? Burning down houses? It would explain the fact that they have money and the insurance fraud, right?* He asked her if she meant insurance that might pay off on land they might own. *Yes. I mean, if his brother is doing this, it only stands to reason that he knows, and why not make a little off his addiction?*

*Christ.* Mason didn't come any closer, but she could see that he wanted to. Not only that, but she was sure that given the chance, he might shake the shit out of Howard and make him tell him everything there was to know. Like where the stash was.

*I think we should go about our business and let him go.* He asked her why. *Because he's not going to help us find his brother, I'm sure of it. And even if he did, the most we could hope for is he gets taken away and his brother runs again. I'm betting we won't find him at all if he does.*

*All right. But I've called Paddy. He's going to have one of his men follow him, and he's going to have someone watch wherever Vance is. I don't want either of them running, but I certainly don't want the mill to go up in flames, or one of our homes.* She agreed with him, and the others walked away. *I don't know if I'd tell him not to tell his brother he talked to you. If he doesn't know your name, he might not know anyway. But just be careful with him. I'm not going anywhere until he's gone.*

Gerard didn't go far either, and the two of them, Mason and Gerard, stood close enough that if Howard did anything at all, he'd be dead in seconds.

She smiled up at the man now, knowing a bit more about him. He looked so innocent, she wondered if he knew how his brother was getting him into trouble.

"I have to go inside now." He nodded, and she smiled again. "I'm having dinner with some people about some things. Maybe we can see each other tomorrow. You could meet me for lunch or dinner."

"You mean like a date?" She said she'd like that. "I never been on one before, but I don't have no money."

"I'll take care of it. You can buy next time." He nodded and told her he should have the stash for his brother by then. "Good. Okay. I'll see you tomorrow. At the diner. You want to meet for lunch then?"

"Sure. Lunch. I like lunch."

After she left him, she knew that lunch with this man wasn't going to be just the two of them. She had a feeling that the entire FBI and her family were going to be there as well.

# CHAPTER 10

"This is…it's…." Gerard looked at Susie, then the contract again. "This is a joke, right? You did this because you thought it would be funny. I think it's funny, don't you, Susie? It's funny, right? I think it's…it's funny."

"It's not funny, and I worked hard for that, young man." Ed laughed, his good humor almost sucking him into their fun. "You'll get the rest of the money when the horses are picked up. Which will be in about a week. I know that's not a lot of time, and he knows that, but you—"

"I think this has gone far enough." Gerard stood up, then sat back down. His hand was tangled up in Susie's, and she seemed to be frozen in place. "I mean, I want to make some money off these horses too. They're eating a lot more than cattle do, and we have to put a roof on the barn. That's what we were hoping for."

"You got that." Todd laughed as he handed him the thick file that had been in front of him. "This is what you can expect from Rose. And trust me, Gerard, this one is as real as the one that Ed gave you."

With shaking fingers, he opened the file. He could see the check, just as the other one, had been attached to the front of the contract. Gerard looked over at Susie when she squeaked. If it wasn't so unmanly like, he might have done the same thing. As it was, he was having a hard time holding down his dinner. Susie took the check with trembling hands before she spoke to them.

"This is for over three million dollars. Three million. With the other check...I'm with Gerard on this one. This is a joke. No way did these two men just pay us seven million dollars for a couple of dozen horses each." Ed told Susie that it was only a start for Jackson. "You're not helping."

"Honey, I'm trying to help you. You have—and I'm paraphrasing here—you have the finest stock of pure blooded race animals he's ever seen. Not only that, but he's going to tell some of his other competition what he got and where he got them. He figures that he got the best of the best, and they can have the rest. He also wants to be notified as soon as you get new stock in."

Gerard wondered if there was any more new stock to be had when Susie spoke again.

"What if he gets these horses back to his stables, or whatever they're called, and they turn out to be duds? Is he going to sue us?"

Todd answered her this time. "No. It's part of the contract. He can't even bad mouth you to others because he picked the horses himself. It's not like you told him which to pick. Also, Rose wants the same deal. You get in more horses and he wants to be notified. I have been talking with Ed, and we think that these two men are the only ones we'll give this deal to. The rest, well, they can be notified, but only after Rose and Jackson have had what they want out of the deal." Todd looked at Gerard as he continued. "You're going to make a killing off this venture. And there are some things...some that you've been made aware of, and others I would very much like for you to think about. The bed and breakfast for starters."

"I have something to add on that." Gerard had been talking to his brother Darin on their way there. "I've changed my mind on that. I think that they should purchase one of the older buildings downtown and convert it. There is one in particular that will suit, I think. It has nine floors, and it could be renovated to accommodate six businessmen and their staff. Also, I think that the lower floor, the one on the ground floor, should be a nice restaurant. One that caters to large groups of people, and has a few tables for other guests. High-end food, with a staff that will give them all the room that they need."

"Who would rent an entire floor to come to this town?" Susie flushed when she looked at him. Her voice had been high and loud, and he knew just how she felt. They were well and truly over their heads with this. "Look, I'm not sure this is a good idea. I have a feeling this is going to go downhill fast."

Todd turned his computer toward them as he explained. "There are fourteen emails from men just like Rose and Jackson that want to come and have a look-see — their words not mine — at the horses. Three had expressed an interest in taking as many as a couple of dozen, and there is one that is coming from across the world to see them."

Gerard felt his head start to spin, and he felt his dinner begin to feel very lead like. Before he knew it, he was facing his feet and someone was holding him down.

"I'm all right now." Mason growled at him to shut up. "I'm really okay. Let me up, please."

When his hand moved, Gerard sat up. They were all staring at him as if he was going to explode or something, so he just grinned. This wasn't something he wanted anyone to witness, and knew for as long as he lived, he'd be teased about fainting like a little girl.

"I've never been a millionaire before." Everyone laughed, and he looked at Susie. "You did this. All of this. I don't know how to thank you for…for just being my mate. I love you."

Gerard was feeling sort of sappy, and when he kissed Susie on the mouth, the room cheered him on. But he wasn't all right, not really. Christ, he really was a millionaire, and he had no idea what to do. Emma congratulated him, and his brothers teased him just in general, but inside, his belly was making all sorts of protests.

As they talked about what was going to need to be done for the next cattle drive, he tried to pay attention. In a week, he and his brothers were going to go two states over to bring in three hundred head of cattle that Zach had gotten for nearly nothing. It looked like they were going to have to get some help with the run, and it was mentioned that Paddy and a few of his men should come with them.

"Do you take a chuck wagon?" Ed only smiled when they all stared at him and his question. "I've never been on one, and I've only seen what they do on television. Is it any different?"

"We do take a chuck wagon, as a matter of fact. It's mostly filled with convenient stuff. Coffee and some clothing. We have a portable shower too. Things just to make it easier on us. Someone will go into a town along the way and meet us for dinner with food that has been cooked and ready for us. Usually there are about five or six men or women that run it. It's not as high tech as some of them, but it beats cooking over an open flame every night, and eating nothing more than a few cans of whatever was there and some jerky. Which travels well, but tastes nothing like meat." Mason smiled at he continued. "We're going to be gone for about a week and a half and, trust me, no one wants my brothers to have a shower more than I do."

"What about things like bathrooms?" No one answered Emma, and she seemed to get it. "Ah. Men can do it standing up."

"Honey, there are a lot of things that men can do standing up. But it's more fun with a mate." Aunt Georgie hit Jace on the back of the head, and he kissed her on the cheek as he finished talking to Emma. "But seriously. It's not as bad as it looks on television. We hope for good weather and usually get rain if it's summer. It's easier to do in the cooler time of year, not as much dust or rain. Water is a big factor. It's dry going, and the cattle and the horses need more."

"With this many cattle coming with us, we're going to need to take our time. It's not like we might have a stampede or anything, but with county and state roads all over the place, we have to be careful of strays getting into a town and causing some damage." Gerard was feeling better as he continued. "You'd not believe the paperwork involved in coming near a town. The police need to be notified, as well as any local farms. We have to be careful not to trespass on a ranch where our cattle might get mixed with theirs. All kinds of things to worry about as you do this. Railway is better for most of the things we've mentioned, but it's also expensive. Especially if you're only going as far as we are with this herd."

They talked about the cattle and the ranches. The McBrides were due back before the cattle run, and they wondered if he'd want to come with them. Gerard hated to leave Susie, but she said that she had plenty to keep her busy, and they both could talk all the time should they need each other. And Paddy was going to have some of his men around if there was trouble.

He thought of the conversation he and Mason had had with the big wolf. He was nearly in tears when he told them how the men had gotten by him. He'd lost three of his men that day, and two of them had small children. They'd had their throats cut and were left to die all alone, for no reason other than some bastard thought he was in the right.

That was when Mason told him what they'd worked out about his missing pantry food. Gerard had been lucky in figuring it out. Had he not been there when the sale had happened, a lot of things might have gone wrong. As it was, the wolf had been arrested.

"He was stealing it to make your wife look bad. And selling it to the local places for next to nothing gave him some pocket money, he said. His wife was in on it too. I'm not sure what you're to do about something like this, but you should know that the diner had no idea."

Gerard picked up where Mason left off. "He came in the back door, like the regular delivery guy does. He told them that for special runs he had to use his own car…that's how he explained not having a truck. The produce and other items were not selling well in the warehouse, he'd told them, and he could cut them a deal. Margaret, the owner of the diner, said it really helped them out a few times to have some extra around like he'd brought them."

"He'll be shunned." Gerard knew that would happen. His family would be thrown out of the pack too. And the male would be marked, a mark that would never heal on him so long as Paddy was alive. "He'll also lose it all. His home, his status. How could he do this to us? To his pack."

Gerard told him what the man had told him. "He said that you were hanging with us too much, and that he needed for you to see what it was going to cost you to have us as friends."

"I should simply kill them. Both of them. But not...not with the other deaths. I can't do that." Both he and Mason said they understood. "Thank you. I'm in your debt for helping me out. I'll think of some way to repay you too."

And now they were going over what had happened the day that his men were killed yet again. The pack was having some major issues, and if things didn't start to turn around soon, it was going to fall apart, and Paddy might be killed.

"I was talking to Colbert when he was murdered by that bastard. We were talking about the way his little girl was coming up on her tenth birthday. She was going to get herself a new haircut, and her momma was taking her to get her nails done. A girly thing, he called it. Then he was just...I never had someone so close to me die before. I mean my parents, yeah, but to be having a conversation with someone and it just end was...it was too much for this old man."

Gerard felt like finding Benjamin and killing him again. As it was now, no one would ever find even a bone fragment of either man. They had been dealt with pack style.

Gerard was surprised, but Susie only smiled as she watched Palmer walk to the love of his life. Aunt Georgie deserved this. Hell, they both did. And when he went down on one knee in front of her, Aunt Georgie was nodding even before he asked her. They were going to be very happy together, Gerard thought.

After dinner was cleared away, they talked about what to do with Vance and his brother. Logan was going to go over the building to find where the money might be. He had a nice metal detector that he'd been wanting to use since it came in. And Zach and Darin were going to see if they could find out how long Vance had been here in town. Everyone had assumed that he'd left the country, but apparently he'd been right under their noses all along. Todd said he'd make some calls now, and left them to do so.

Gerard told his family he and Susie had to get home. They were going to walk around town for a little while, he and Susie. They wanted to walk by the building that Darin was talking about and think about what he'd been telling them. Gerard hadn't thought of the money anymore, because every time he did, he got a little tense. When they were alone, he asked Susie about it.

"I'm not sure what to think." He smiled at her when she laughed. "It's a lot to take in, don't you think? I mean, I'm still having trouble just thinking all those zeroes are real. And we have two checks with that many on it."

"I know what you mean. With you, I don't feel so overwhelmed, but I'm telling you, for a while there, I thought for sure I was going to puke or pass out. I'm glad I did the latter of the two." She laughed with him as they made their way in the back of the empty building. "Todd seems to think this is only the beginning. Do you think so too?"

"I don't know. I'm not really ready to think in those terms yet. I would like to try our hand at being rich. Buy the building, this building, and have it changed up. Even if this thing doesn't work out, we'll have something to rent out should the town need it." He liked that idea.

The building wasn't in terrible shape, but it was pretty dirty. The windows had been broken on the lower levels, and someone, the city more than likely, had put up boards all around it. The police, Mason told them, had been making it a habit of running the homeless out, and Landon was working on a homeless shelter for them just on the outskirts of town. He supposed that when the man returned, he'd be right back on that project too.

As they made their way up the stairs to the second, then the third level, he could see what his brother meant. This would make a great suite for a meeting, as well as a nice comfortable hotel.

There were hardwood floors on each level that would need some pretty intense sanding. The windows would need to be replaced with something more efficient, and the furnace would be upgraded, with air added too. He doubted that this place would be all that cool in the heat of the summer. Then there was the plumbing.

"He said that a bedroom and bath could be put on each floor, with a sort of kitchenette. Then a bigger area could be made so it would accommodate business meetings should they need them, as well as anything else that they might need. They'd be pricey, I guess. It's going to take a lot of work." Gerard nodded, thinking of what the dirty hardwood floors would look like when they were sanded and polished up. "I love his idea about how to use the lower level; the street level could be a sort of shop and restaurant for the public…and for if they needed food up here, like he said."

"I can see that too. Not a shop with things in it from all over the world, but local things. Things made by some of the people around here." Susie said she loved it. "And so you know, I don't ever want to have a dude ranch out there or here."

She laughed, and he moved toward her. "You're very sexy right now. I'm thinking that perhaps we could see if there is any place we can see if your cat is hungry. Maybe play around a little while the place is empty. What do you think?" He actually staggered a little. "Is he, Gerard? Is your cat hungry for his mate?"

He nearly let him take him, but they were miles from their house and going home as a cat could get him killed. While there were a lot of shifters in this town, there were still a great many humans that he'd have to walk by to get there. And being a naked human would be no less troublesome.

Gerard took off his shirt. He nearly dropped it on the floor, but hung it from a nail on a post next to him, and then took off his pants and boxers and hung them as well. His shoes he kicked off, and left his socks on to make his way to her. When she started to take off her blouse, he stopped her.

"I want to do it. Let me undress you so I can touch you all over." She nodded and raised her hands above her head and held onto the post behind her. "You have no idea how much I want to taste every inch of you. Take my time with making you come. I want to drink from you, get my fill of you. Then I want to fuck you. Take you hard while you're standing there dripping wet for me."

"I'd like that too." He opened her blouse up, taking the buttons from the holes slowly, peeling it away from her skin as he kissed the exposed area. When it was open, he moaned when she cupped his cock in her hand, and he rocked hard against her. "I want to feel you coming down my throat again. The taste of you is never enough for me."

"Not this time. You offered yourself to us and we want you." Nodding, she put her hands back up to the post. He wanted to beg her to touch him again, but he moved to his knees to take off her pants. "Do you have any idea how delicious you smell right now? And the more of you I see, the stronger your scent becomes for me. You're like a drug. I can't get enough of you."

He pulled her pants down after opening the snap and pulling the zipper down with his teeth. Her moans were fueling him, her scent driving his cat wild. He moved along his skin, taking him along his arms, his hands changing to claws that bit into her skin. Gerard wasn't sure how much longer he could hold him as he pulled her panties off. Dropping them on the floor, he let his cat consume him.

Not able to hold him back from taking what he'd been promised, his cat lunged at her. He was licking her pussy, lapping quickly at the juices that streamed down her thighs. Even as Susie spread her legs for him, he knew that it wasn't enough. The cat, like him, wanted her all. When he nipped at her thigh, Gerard cautioned him to be careful with her, but the moment his teeth sank into her leg, he knew that he was marking her as his own.

The crush of bones made him wince. The sound of her screams had him begging him to let her go. But he held her in his mouth, almost as if he were thinking to change her. The power of what he was doing, the feel of something going on other than just her blood going down his throat, made Gerard moan. It was scrumptious…the only word he could think of to describe what he was tasting from her.

When he sealed the wound, his cat licked her pussy again before simply letting go. It had never happened that way with his cat before. He would usually have to take him, but this time, the cat simply let go of his human and he sat on his knees.

Gerard looked at the scar forming on her thigh now. It was a perfect imprint of teeth. The sharp incisors were there, the upper and lower jaw line outlined against her pale flesh. No blood marred the skin…a little bruising, but it, too, was going away as Gerard leaned down and kissed it.

"Please, I need to come with you." He moved his mouth up her leg, to the juncture at her thighs that seemed to beg for him to take her. She came, screaming, her juices flooding his mouth. Even as he slid his fingers into her, she tightened around him as her next climax took her.

He fucked her, ate her until she was wobbly on her feet. He hadn't had enough of her and wasn't sure that he would ever have as much as he wanted. Standing up, helping her to hang on, he lifted her up by her ass and slammed his cock deep into her. This time he didn't pause to let her adjust to him. He didn't wait to see if she was ready for him. He took it. And took it hard.

Her nails dug deep into his arms. Susie's face was rapturous in her release. He held her, enthralled with her beauty, knowing that he'd never see anything as lovely as she was at that moment. When she looked at him, her eyes dark with her need, he pressed her against the post again and fucked her slowly.

"You're so tight around me. My cock can feel every muscle of your sheath. Every tightening of your pussy around me makes me weak with the need to empty inside of you." Her nod, short and breathless, made him smile. "When I come in you, I want you to mark me. I need to feel owned by you, possessed by the woman that I love."

"Yes. Please." He fucked her harder, his body vibrating with the need to come. When he felt his spine tingle, a feeling that came over him a lot lately when he was with Susie, he knew that he was close. Tilting his head for her, he felt her mouth on his throat, her breath heating his already hot skin, and then her teeth scrape none too gently over his pulse. When her teeth took a small nip, breaking the skin but not tearing into it, he fucked her again, his body no longer caring about anything but filling her.

His climax took his breath away. For several seconds, no longer than that, his heart stopped beating, as if poised on the edge of life or death. And when Susie bit him, tearing deeply into his throat as if to take his life, Gerard cried out as another, equally powerful climax took him.

Lights danced behind his eyelids. Nerve endings seemed to vibrate and tingle every part of his skin and body. The roar of his blood echoed in his ears, and he even heard his hair move on his head as he leaned his head on the post behind them.

There was nothing left of him to move. He was literally drained of energy and anything else that might have helped him stand. Laughing slightly, he held her in his arms and tried to think how he could get them both to the floor without dropping her or falling on his ass while trying to do it.

"I think you killed me." He lifted his head just enough to look at her. Focusing on her was an issue, but it didn't matter as his hearing seemed to be coming back on line. "I've never felt...good lord, Gerard, what did you do to me?"

"Me? Oh baby, that was all you." She grinned at him, and he wondered if she was in better shape than he was. He didn't even have the energy for even that small task. "I think I want to sit down, but I don't think I can do that and not drop us both on our asses."

She giggled at him, and he felt better. There was something so loving about hearing her giggle that he wanted to make her do it again. When he was rested. Closing his eyes again, he leaned on the post. When she shifted enough that he had to let her go, he felt her body lean onto his then turn him so that his back was to the post.

"We should head home." He nodded, not moving. "Gerard, it's late. We need to get home. Come on, you can do it."

"No. I don't think I can. I think you just let me stay here and let me die with my dignity. I think I've been put to shame by you." He opened one eye when something hit him in the face. "Yes. I suppose my drained body should be found with clothing on. My aunt won't be so shamed if I'm dressed."

"You're being weird." He pulled his shirt on, feeling a little better all the time. When his pants hit him in the same way that his shirt had, he thought about what they'd just done. Or as a matter of fact, what she'd done to him. "Are you getting dressed or not?"

"What did you do to me?" She asked him what he meant. "My cat. He bit you, and I swear that I felt something. Like a shift or something."

"I don't know what you mean. But if you're taking about how it made me feel being bitten by your cat, then you're right. That was pretty amazing." He didn't think that was it but didn't say anything as he pulled on his pants. Christ, he really was zapped. "Do you think we should do what your brother said and renovate this building? I guess we could use it for about anything else if it fails or turns out to be not needed for meetings and stuff."

"I don't know. I mean, yes, we should buy the building, but even if the horses don't turn out to be as big a deal as everyone thinks, we can always rent the place out for meetings. And I like the idea of having a restaurant on the lower levels. This area can always use a couple of different places to eat."

He took her hand in his as they walked down the stairs again. He could see all kinds of things that would work in his building should the hotel of sorts not work out. And he voiced them to Susie.

"I can see that. A nice place for shops on the levels. That would mean having the elevators working. I don't think they do." He told her they did work, but they were a little dirty. "Okay. Let's do it. So long as if that room is ever empty we can go back up there and have some more fun."

He didn't tell her that he thought it might kill him if they did, and decided that he was going to start running more. There was no way he was going to be that weak after sex again. And by the time they got home, he had an entire list of things he was going to do to get into better shape. Gerard was going to be the most fit of all his family even if it killed him.

# CHAPTER 11

"Can you and Gerard meet me at the mill?" Susie handed the phone to Gerard. There was something about his voice, something so...she supposed it sounded like he was afraid and it made her cat nervous too. And when Gerard said nothing for several minutes, she had a feeling that it wasn't just scary, but really bad. And when he hung up the phone a few minutes later, she watched him as he just sat there.

"They found Howard. He was in the back of the mill near the loading doors when Logan and a couple of other men went to unload another truck. Someone had cut his throat." Susie nodded, her heart breaking for the man. "It must have happened some time during the night, of course, but Logan seems to think that it happened only an hour ago. He can still smell fresh blood."

"Do they know who did it?" He shook his head. "The police don't know who did it, or Logan doesn't know who did it?"

"The police." That scared her too, and she got up and put the dishes they were using for breakfast in the sink. She'd been washing the dishes up as she went and the water was still hot. As she scrubbed them, Gerard came up behind her and wrapped his arms around her waist. He held her to his body as he continued. "Logan said that he can smell the man who did it to him, and he knows it was Vance. He said that the police are looking into all kinds of things, but he thinks maybe he killed his brother because he mentioned us."

"So I should have let Mason bring him in. It's my fault." He turned her around so quickly that she nearly dropped the plate she had in her hand. "I should have listened to him, and now a man is dead because of — "

"Stop it right now." Her eyes filled with tears when he kissed her. "You had nothing to do with this. You didn't cut his throat. You're not the one that tried to burn down our home, and you certainly had nothing to do with either him or his brother trying to take our family farm. These men were and are criminals. That had nothing to do with what happened to him. It's sad, yes. But nothing to do with us."

He held her while she cried. Gerard was right, she'd not done it to the man, but he was dead all the same. When Gerard told her that he had to go into town, she asked if she needed to go as well.

"No. You can stay here. I'm sure you can stay out of trouble for a few hours." Susie smacked him on the arm. "Just be careful, all right? Don't be trying to take on men that are bigger than you. I'm sure you're meaner, but they don't know that. And if you need someone, Paddy is still around the land."

"I'll be fine."

When he left a few minutes later, she cleaned up the kitchen from their breakfast, then put on her boots to go to the barn. She'd gotten into the habit of putting her knife in her boot, as it was easier to get out from there than from her pants. As she pulled on Gerard's jacket against the cold morning snow, she thought of what all she had to do today.

In a few days the horses from the Rose farm were being picked up, and she wanted to make sure that they were bathed and brushed. She didn't know why it mattered, but it did to her. It was the day that the men were supposed to have left, but they were delaying things for a few days. Mason said that he wanted to see how they did this move of all these horses, and she was sort of excited about it too. The Jackson farm was coming in two days later to get their horses.

There were a couple of men in the barns when she walked in. Two she knew from around the ranches, and Paddy was there as well. He introduced her to the men that had come out to help her today. Then he asked to speak to her about something as the men scattered off to work. Soon it was just the two of them. She moved to the doorway of the barn when the stallion that she'd first talked to came running up to them from the paddock. Susie thought it was the wolf that made him nervous, but then she realized he was running at them, not away.

"What is it, boy? You get yourself spooked?"

Something hard fell against her from behind, and she turned to see what it was when something touched the back of her head. The horse in front of her was so agitated that it was all she could do to keep her cat under control. When the holder of the gun spoke, she immediately reached for Gerard.

"You're going to come with me." She told Garth that she wasn't and glanced down at Paddy. He was bleeding from the head, and she started to lean down to him when the man behind her hit her with what she thought was a gun. "You're not going to fuck around with me. I have a gun. Now, I want you to get in the car and take me to the bank. Then when I get money, you're going to run me to the airport and make sure I get on the plane with no problems."

"You don't have any money, you moron. How do you suppose you're going to get any money from the bank? I'm pretty sure they're looking for you anyway." He hit her again, and she saw stars. Gerard told her he was on his way, and she told him to hurry. Then she told him about Paddy when he asked where he was.

*Christ. We were almost to the mill. Mason and the others are in town, but are coming as well. Aunt Georgie is on her way with Emma. Holly is calling the police.* She told him she was okay, but if he hit her again, all bets were off. *He's going to pay for that.*

*Be calm.* He told her that he couldn't be fucking calm. *Yes, you can. If you're a cat when you get here and the police are here, who do you think they'll shoot first?*

He growled at her. *I hate it when you're all logical and shit.* She had to laugh and felt a little calmer because of it. *Good girl. Just keep your head on you and we'll be there soon. Aunt Georgie said that she's coming up from the south side.*

*I don't see her.* She looked in that direction. Then it occurred to her that she was looking for Georgie, not her cat. As Garth shoved her away from the fence and toward Gerard's truck, she wished now that Zach hadn't picked him up and Gerard had taken his own car.

They were both in the truck, the gun pointed at her, when she realized she'd have to go in the house and get the keys. For some reason, he thought that was stupid that they didn't leave their keys in their cars when they were in the driveway. He asked her why they were in the house. She shook her head before answering his stupid question.

"Oh, I don't know. Because of idiotic morons like you." This time when he hit her, it was in the face. As her head was knocked sideways, she saw the huge cougar coming at her. Her own, on the edge since this man had come up behind her, simply took her.

He scrambled to get away from her. Susie had had enough of this kind of shit happening to her, but only sat on the seat next to him and snarled. When she swiped her paw at him, cutting him across the face, he screamed like she'd cut him worse. There would be a scar, of course, but she'd not hurt him enough to kill him. Yet, anyway.

"Let me out. Let me out." She wondered if he thought she was holding him somehow when he was right there by the fucking door. "What the fuck are you? You just…fucking bitch, what are you?"

Snarling at him made him scream again. Watching Georgie go into the barn, she wondered if she was going to see to Paddy. And when two men came out with her and helped their alpha up, she watched them walk toward the truck. As soon as one of the men knocked on the glass on Garth's side, he screamed again. He was the biggest baby she'd ever seen.

It took them several seconds to get him to roll down the window. The men were laughing and having a grand time, and Susie thought what the hell, she might as well too, and laid her head on the leg of Garth. His screams were getting on her nerves, and Paddy, at the window that had been opened, told him to shut up. With a small whimper, Garth finally did.

"Now see what you gone and did?" Garth told him to let him out. "No, I don't think so. I like you right fine where you are. She's going to ask you a few questions, and you either answer them right, honest and true, or so help me, I'll tell her to tear your throat out."

Garth looked at her, his body pressed hard against the door, but he only nodded. The screaming was done for now, she supposed, and she nearly laughed when he begged her not to hurt him. Georgie spoke to her just as she was thinking of touching him with her paw again.

*Oh honey, not just yet. I'm having a hard enough time just not laughing at the fool man. If he wets himself, I'll just lose it. I swear I will.* She told her she was having the same issues. *Now. I can talk to Paddy here and he can relay the questions or whatever to this idiot. Have you met a stupider human?*

*No. Not in a long time. Ask him if he killed his brother, to start with.*

Paddy nodded after a couple of seconds and asked Garth if he had.

"My brother was a moron. Why did he have to tell you what we were doing anyway?" She did put her paw on his thigh, and was happy when she saw him piss his pants. "Please don't hurt me. Christ, you're a fucking animal, and all of you are going to pay for this."

"You think so? From where I'm standing, you don't have a pot to piss in." Paddy looked at Garth's groin, then up at her. "Well, I guess he don't even have any piss to put in said pot, now does he?"

She was having a blast and asked if he had the money. As the question was being asked again, she reached out to Gerard to tell him she was all right and what they were doing.

*Aunt Georgie is keeping us informed and entertained. Logan has slowed to a normal speed, and Mason has as well, he told me. Sounds like you have it under control. Oh, and the police are on their way. Aunt Georgie can still talk to Paddy, but she's going to go to the house and shift and put on clothing before they get there.*

*You, however, are going to have to think of something. I don't want to have to visit you in the jail.*

*There might be a nice post you can hang me from at night when you come for some conjugal visits.* He laughed and she looked at Paddy. *I think I need to pay attention here. I'll see you soon.*

"He wants to know if you're going to kill him or not. Personally, I'd be afraid of getting nasty from his smell. Might be that he'll shit himself in a bit, and that'll be funny too." She told Paddy through Georgie to behave. "I'm not the one sitting in the car with him. Could be that he's gonna do it there, and that man of yours, he's not going to be too happy."

"I want you to tell this bitch to let me go and we'll go our separate ways. I want my money and then I don't care what she does." She told Paddy to tell Garth that they already had the money. "You do not. Howard told me you had no idea where it was. I'm the only one that knows now."

Before she could think about what she might be doing, Susie put her paw on his leg again and dug deep into his flesh. He screamed this time as blood pooled under his leg. Susie reached into his mind to see if she could, and got a great deal more than she'd bargained for. Then she got what she wanted and pulled back just as someone came to her side of the car and opened the door. She took off to the house as she reached for Gerard again.

*The money is in the beam over the counter where the cash register used to be. There is piece of wood that doesn't look like the rest of the wood, and it's latched with a nail that sticks from the upper flooring. Move it gently, as there is a gun there as well.* He asked her what the gun was used for. *Garth killed two men with it, and Howard was to have thrown it in the river, but he liked it. I guess he told his brother before he killed him.*

*You know this?* She told him what she'd done. *Don't tell anyone. I don't...please, just don't tell anyone and I'll figure this out.*

*You're angry?* He told her no, but he needed to talk to her first. *What is it? What's happened, Gerard?*

*I was sitting here minding my own business when I just...Logan was telling me he was all right. I know that he's been sort of down lately and I've been worried about him, so I playfully punched him in the arm. I felt him, Susie. All of his thoughts and emotions. Not like a connection that we as cougars have, but actually felt them.* She told him that was what she felt when she had touched Garth, and the connection that she had with the animals. *That day in the building. I knew that something more had happened than the greatest sex I've ever had. We became one, I think.*

As soon as she was in the house, she paused in pulling on a pair of panties. She'd pulled on her bra and shirt already, and was glad that when she sat down, the bed was close enough to catch her. Susie tried to think what to say to him.

*You felt his emotions, but they were stronger, right? Like they were yours. Not like another leap member, but his pain and happiness that was there.* He said yes. *And you know things...a lot of things that you might not have been told.*

*I know that when he was ten years old he thought that he'd found his mate. A little girl in his class that was murdered a few months later in a car accident. Logan thinks that...he's sure that his mate is dead. It's what has him avoiding us and my other two brothers. He will...he thinks he'll never have what we have.*

*But you know better.* Gerard said that he did. *It's what I can do. Not just what...I could never touch a human before and read them. I did that today.*

*You think this has to do with last night? And what happened when I bit you? I do, but I'd really like to hear what you think as well.* She heard the police pull into the yard and looked out the window as she finished dressing. She wasn't sure how to answer Gerard so said nothing to him. He seemed to understand. *We're nearly there, love. We'll talk when this shit is settled with Vance.*

She told him she was going outside now and that she'd not say a word about anything. *Gerard, what does this mean? You think that we're the same now?*

*Yes.*

She stepped out on the porch just as two police officers were pulling Garth from the truck. Even from where she was, she could smell him. Not only had he wet himself, but apparently he'd crapped his pants too. She looked over at Paddy when he laughed at the antics near the truck. The man was having a great deal of fun for someone who had gotten his head pounded not twenty minutes ago. Susie couldn't help but smile too.

"They don't want to be touching him. Can't blame them a bit, nope. He's stinking it to high heaven." She asked him what he'd done. "Oh nothing much. But none of them officers there are going to believe a word that he says to them. I'm thinking he'll be in a loony bin in short order."

She listened to Vance then, screaming about cougars as big as he was, women changing into cats and threatening to drive him over the edge. She wasn't sure what edge he was talking about, but Paddy was right. No one believed a word he said.

"She cut me open. Look at this." The closest officer backed away from Garth when he pulled his torn pants up nearly to his balls. "She nearly unmanned me. Why aren't you arresting her right now?"

"You're telling me a woman, Mrs. Douglas here, turned into a cat...a cougar, and tried to kill you?" Garth said that he'd seen her do it. The officer looked at her, then back at Garth before shaking his head. "You on something there, Mr. Vance? Maybe you might hit your head or something?"

"I did no such thing. Ask her. She was supposed to drive me into the bank, but the fucking bitch had no keys." The officer asked him why he was going to the bank just as the Douglas men pulled into the drive. Gerard walked to her, but the rest of them stayed near their cars. She didn't know what was going on until he spoke to her.

"They're making sure that he doesn't get away. I'm thinking that he might try to get them to let him go if nothing else. Mason has no idea who else is in his pocket. Also, they don't know that he killed his brother." She nodded. "Besides, they're hoping the police do let him go so they can have their fun."

Susie didn't want to think of the fun they might be having with this man, but she did know that whatever it might be, he'd not enjoy it nearly as much as they did. As Garth continued to tell them what she'd done, Susie leaned back on Gerard and tried her best not to think of what was going on between the two of them.

~~~

Gerard knew that he was going to confess about everything soon. All Vance talked about was how Susie had done this or that to him, and that she'd told him things that Gerard knew weren't true. He even alluded to the fact that she might have been the one that hit Paddy when he'd told them about being ambushed by Garth.

"I just want you to explain to me why you wanted Mrs. Douglas to take you to the bank. Don't you know that you're wanted for some things that have been going on around town? I'm pretty sure you couldn't have missed it, what with it being all over the news and what not." Gerard watched Cort, one of the town's officers. Cortland Anderson and he had gone to school together, and as far as he knew the man was much smarter than he was projecting at the moment. "You said that just before she turned into this here dog that she was going to take you—"

"Not a dog, you fool. A cougar. Why the hell are you still holding me like this when she's the animal around here? And as for the bank, she was going to give me some money. I needed to get away." Cort asked him where he was going. "I'm not stupid enough to think that you're not going to arrest me sooner or later."

"Arrest you for what?"

Vance growled, and Susie laughed. It was funny, the way he growled like it was going to make a difference, but when he lunged at her, Gerard punched him in the face as hard as he could. No one moved when he hit the dirt. As he lay there, Gerard had a moment of pure fear. He might have killed the man. But when he moaned, Gerard let out his breath. Christ, that had been close.

A wagon, a large unpadded van, was brought in for Garth, and he fought them as he was being loaded in. When he broke free of them, going for the tree line, Zach took him to the ground with a full bodied tackle, something akin to what he'd done on the field when they played ball for the high school. He held him there with a boot to his chest. The officers were just picking Garth up when he started yelling about what he'd done.

"He told them. Damn it all to fuck. Why am I the bad guy here? You know as well as I do that Rogers did this. I was just a pawn in his scheme. Of course, it was my idea, but he just took it and ran with it." Cort asked him what he was talking about. "The plan to take the ranches, you fucking idiot. We were going to make a killing off this land,

and he got us all caught. Then Howard. That stupid halfwit just had to tell them what we were doing. And now look. He's dead because of it. I should have killed him before last night, and I'd have all the fucking money."

"What money?" Garth looked at Gerard and laughed. "You don't have any money, Garth. All you have is a lot of people pissed off at you for robbing them."

"Shit, you mean like you? Fuck that shit. You didn't deserve the money, and now look at you. You all have it. Well, I'll have mine soon enough, and I'm going to do what my brother was going to do. Buy me an island and live there so no one can touch me." Garth was being stuffed into the back of the van again when he started spouting off about the men he'd killed. "That man that thought he could just come in here and take what was mine is now rotting in a grave on the McBride ranch. Go dig him up and see him. Put a bullet in his head just as neatly as I sliced open Howard's throat. Hated to do it, but he never learned to shut up."

He told them about the second man too. The banker that had been there before Rogers had been. He'd been shot too, and his body was buried in the cemetery. It might take them awhile to find him, Garth told them, as he'd done a number on him by tossing his body into the fertilizer pit at the back of the property, the one they used for the flowers in the summer. He was still laughing as the doors were being closed.

"Man, that man can carry on." Cort turned to him with his hand out. "I really appreciate you calling us in on this, Gerard. Been looking for this little turd for some time now. I hear tell you and the Mrs. have some horse selling going on."

"We do. There are some buyers from down south coming up to pick them up on Monday." Cort nodded, and as soon as Gerard touched his hand to the officer, he felt the same emotions that he had with his brother. It nearly took him to his knees. "Cort, you should…you should bring the family out and let them see them. Some of them are very gentle. Maybe your son can…he can have a ride on one."

Cort stared at him, then looked away. "Who told you? I mean…well, hell, anyone could have, I guess. We thought we could take…it's hard, you know? Trying to do this on our own. My wife's mom helps when she can, but she don't like to come over as much as she used to. It's draining us all, and our resources are about gone too. They don't give him much longer. Less than a year, I guess. He's only five, for Christ's sake. Too young to…." When he sobbed just standing there next to him and Susie, Gerard felt his heart break for the man. His five-year-old little boy was dying.

Gerard only nodded, wanting and needing to help him but not sure how. To have your child dying as his was, cancer taking him at such a young age, Gerard wanted to pull him into his arms and hold him for a little while.

"You bring him on out here and we'll set him up on one of the ponies. There are a lot of them." Cort nodded but still hadn't looked at him. "I'm sorry. I wish I could do more."

"He's been wanting to come out since he heard you had them. I told him that…I was gonna ask you in a few days if he could…it's not something we like to do. Ask people for help with him. It puts some people off, you know? Like it's too much for them. They should live in our shoes for a day." Gerard asked him why he'd not asked before. "I guess it's pride. Maybe a little like we don't want to share him in these last few months we have left with him. He's my boy, Gerard. My little boy."

"I can't imagine what you're going through. I am so sorry. But I am serious. Susie and I would love to have you all come out and spend the day with us. We're going on a drive sometime in the next few days, so come out before then. Hell, come out whenever you want. Someone is always here." Cort told him he'd talk to his wife. "You tell her that we insist."

After he left them, Vance on his way to jail and the other officers going back to work, Gerard turned to his brothers and Paddy's pack and smiled.

"Steaks all around. Our treat. It's been a hell of a day and I, for one, could use a nice fun dinner." After the whooping and yelling calmed down, Aunt Georgie started sending men to the store for food, and she and Susie entered the house with the others to get started on the side stuff. Mason patted him on the back and went to the barn with the rest. Gerard sat on the steps and thought about what the fuck had just happened.

Things around here might never be calm, he thought. And realized it was fine. Because without his family, he wasn't sure...he knew that he'd never make it. And with the love of his life in his corner, Gerard thought he could do just about anything. Getting up, he went to the barn. The men were going to show up in the morning to put on the new roof and start on the other buildings as well.

# CHAPTER 12

When their plane touched down, Emma was right there to greet them, excited beyond words to see her mom and dad after so long. A month didn't seem like that to most people, but to her it had seemed like a lifetime or two. As soon as she saw her mom she moved forward, nearly taking down the security officer that was standing by the door when she got there. Her dad was just coming down the steps when she finished hugging her mom.

"You come to meet your old dad, did you?" She said that she was there for Mom, but he was okay to see too. "Hush that now, you know that I'm your favorite."

"Did you bring me anything?" He just smiled at her. It had been their joke, probably for more fathers and daughters than just the two of them, since she'd been a little girl. "I got some news for you too when we get to the car. Things around the ranches have been a little stressful, but we got it handled. Even without you here."

Helping them get their luggage into the new car had been fun. She teased them about having much more than they'd left with, and told them about the boxes that had arrived yesterday. Her mom said that she'd gotten a few things for everyone, and even some things for the new baby. She was busting to tell them about her and Mason, but didn't say anything just yet. Her dad, of course, asked her about her news twice as they were driving to the ranch.

"Not to the house." She knew this and was headed to their home, hers and Masons, even as her mother sounded panicky. "I'm not ready for that just yet. Might not ever be."

"We understand." And Emma did too. Her brother had been...after his death it had been hard for all of them to go to the house. The only person who had been there in the few months he'd been gone was Mason, and that was just to check on things around the inside. There were a number of others moving around and about the ranch at all times, but he wanted to check on the house for them. "We have a place at the house all ready for you. And Georgie has been over baking up a storm. We're having a celebration tomorrow night, so it's good that you came home early."

Only she and Mason knew that her parents had cut their vacation short. It was only five days, but it was enough to know that they wanted to be there for Gerard and Susie. They had contracts for more horses, and they'd hired three more people to work for them fulltime. It was time to have some fun.

"And you should see the building that they're having renovated. The work is going to make that place shine. And they've decided to buy the one next to it too. Just on the off chance that this hotel business works out." Her dad said it would. "You and I know it will, but Susie and Gerard are having a hard time with it. And I think with the money too. They're very rich, but you'd never know it the way that they act. Susie said that they're worried that someone is going to come back and ask for a refund."

"Never been that poor before where I had to worry about money. I can tell you though, it's smart of them to take their time with it. Jumping into too many things will overwhelm their pocket book, as well as themselves. We gonna swing by the building on the way to the house?" She said she could do that. "I'd like to have a look. Just to see what a little gumption can do for a building."

"Palmer has bought two of the buildings too. And he and Georgie are getting married in a few weeks. She finally told us all that he was her mate. I think Mason has known for some time now." Her mother said that she'd thought so too. "I think they're so cute together. They remind me of you two when they think nobody is looking. All in love and stuff."

"I do love your mother. She's the smartest woman I know." Emma grinned at him. "How you like being the mayor? Making them people stand up and take some notice, are you? By golly, you'd better be. You're my daughter and you gotta make me proud."

"I'm working on it, Dad." They drove by the building slowly. He wanted to get out and have a look-see, he said, but they were going to surprise everyone and she knew her father well enough to know that if he got out, he'd be there until the building was finished, offering suggestions and what not. "I have a project I need your help on, Mom. It's about the program that Susie is working on. She is working on a way for handicapped children to come out to the ranch to see and ride horses. And then there are the other animals that she wants to have there too. Mostly shifters that will have more control around them, but she needs help getting the paperwork done correctly."

"She needs to apply for some grants too." Emma told her that Susie would never go for that. "Well, the paperwork will go much smoother if she does it. The government will think they have a hand in it, and that can open more doors than not. I'll talk to her."

Emma could tell that her mom thought it was a done deal then. Katie McBride could open or close more doors than a wind in a door factory. Her dad had been saying that to people for years, and Emma thought it was right. Her mother, for all her quietness and shyness, had more power than the president. Glancing at her dad made her think that Susie didn't stand a chance between these two forces.

As they pulled into the drive of their home, she thought of all the things they'd done to the land since they'd been gone. A barn was being put up at the back of the property for the yard equipment to be stored in. There was also a horse stable for the few horses that Mason had picked out for them. She'd been riding all her life and loved it. Mason had never ridden except for work. She was looking forward to getting him out and in the dark woods.

Then there was the kitchen expansion. The kitchen had been in good shape and large enough for the little entertaining that her grandmother had done, but not for their growing family. When she had great parties—and Emma could remember some pretty fantastic ones when she was younger—Grandma had the food brought to the house and then the mess and all the food taken away when it was done. Randy, their butler, had told her and Mason that it had worked well for her, but cooking in the place now was just not going to work.

"My goodness, child." Her mom laughed when she saw all the men at the house. Seemingly in it, on it, and even under it. They had been working with the house for two weeks now, and she was frankly sick of the construction but could not wait to see it. "What are you doing here? Building a new house?"

"Oh no. Mason and I love this one. We'll never leave. But we needed to make some improvements." Three men came out to get the luggage from the car as she took her parents inside. "The front hall needed new wiring. We plugged in one of those candle things over there and nearly burned the house down around our ears."

She didn't tell them what really happened. That she and Mason had been having sex against the wall, his big cat eating her while she screamed out this name. And when she let her own cat go to take care of his needs, she knocked a large lamp off and it had shattered. But the cord had broken off and the fire from the socket made her cat scream while running for the woods. It had taken her nearly two hours to calm her enough to let her shift back.

There was new furniture too. As well as a television set that was as big as she was. The family had been over to the house twice in recent days to enjoy some football on the big screen, as well as some pretty amazing dinners that Jace had helped make for them.

"You should make this room bigger too." She looked around the office that she'd been using when she and her mom entered it. It was small and lovely, and every time she came in here, she thought of her grandmother. She asked her mom why she thought it should be changed. "She loved this room. I would come in here with her when she was working just to see her here. It suited her, the smallness of it. The colors. You need to make this room yours as well. Something that says 'I'm Emma Douglas, and I love my job.'"

"I do love it." Her mom nodded and sat on the most uncomfortable chair in the entire room. Also the most ugly. "Is Dad going on the run with them?"

"He wants to. But he also doesn't want to step on anyone's toes if he does. He has it in his head that Mason thinks he's too old." They could hear her dad in the kitchen, three rooms from the one they were currently in, talking to the men working in there. She had a feeling she was going to have to increase their pay to have them put up with them. "That man would never make a good librarian. He's too loud, and he thinks that he knows more than the books. I can see him now, telling them stories instead of doing his job. The old poop."

"He's wonderful." Her mom nodded and smiled. "Will you really help Susie? She had this little boy out to her house the other day, and he had so much fun. It wore him out, of course, all the excitement, but his parents were thrilled to death. Cort, that's Gerard's friend and father to little Cort, said that there are hundreds more children that would love to be able to do this before they died. Little Cort has cancer, and they don't give him long to live. Susie cried for two hours after they left. She felt like it wasn't enough, what she'd been able to do for him."

"I'm on a few committees that can help her out too. Some of them are especially there for children and their families. One is the Lasting Wish Foundation. They call it Lasting Wish because it is for them. And their families." Emma knew her mom was on that board and hoped for some help from them as well. "I would suggest that she find herself a photographer. Not for the publication of the photos, but so that the families can have them. It's something that has just started in some of the other places we try to fund. They make these beautiful albums that the parents get as part of their visit. I'm betting that Susie won't want to charge families for this either, will she? I don't know that I would either. It's hard on them, caring for a sick child, and very hard on their bank accounts too. Some have lost their homes over something like this happening."

"No. She won't. I think you're right about that. And Cort and his wife Janie took a lot of pictures. She told me that she might not ever be able to look at them, but she had them if she wanted to." Her mom nodded. "Also, you should know that the money that they found in the mill has been turned over to the FBI. But two days after it was given to them, Susie received a check for double the amount. The agents took up a collection when they heard what she and Gerard were doing, and sent it to them, along with the money from the mill. Some of them know Cort and his wife, and were happy that it could go to help fund a project like this one. I think they ended up giving a lot of it to Cort for medical expenses."

"Good for them. I'm sure that your dad and I will help out as well. We'll start some fund raisers too. Give to the neediest families and help them out. You and I will talk about that later." She nearly pointed out to her mom that Susie wouldn't be happy about getting the money, but didn't. She would let Susie deal with it. "When are you going to tell him?"

"Tell who what?" Her mother only smiled at her. "Seriously, Mom, I don't know what you're talking about."

"The baby." Emma didn't say anything, but put her hand over her still flat belly. "I have known you since before you were born, darling. A mom knows when her little girl is going to have a child of her own. So when are you going to tell your dad?"

"Mason wants to do it. He loves Dad as much as I do. I think he's sort of excited to tell him." Her mom said that her dad loved him as well. "The ranch, it's doing well. Mason is making it work, and he's setting up a meeting as Dad asked him to do with the renters. Did you know that several of them are no longer using the land but still paying rent?"

"No. I had an idea that they weren't, but Landon said that it mattered little to him so long as it was being kept up." Emma shook her head. "They're not?"

"No. Two of the fields have trailers on them. Squatters, Mason thinks. The land isn't set up for that, and they're running water from somewhere via hoses. He said that they're using generators for electricity too." Her mom looked shocked. "Also, there is one tenant that is making noises about taking the land as his own. He claims that Dad gave it to him after he rented it for ten years. Do you know if that's true?"

"The contracts are in your father...in Mason's office. And there is a copy of them filed in the court house. Your dad is very good at that sort of thing. And I know that he'd never give land away. He loves it too much." Emma knew that about her parents, and also knew that the man who was messing with them didn't have a clue who he was fucking with. "You're helping him look into it?"

"Yes. I have filed paperwork to have him removed from the land. As well as the squatters that are abusing it. We don't need someone setting up house there when there is every chance that Mason will expand. Did you know that he'd nearly doubled the amount of steer we have? And the Double Deuce has more cattle on it now than ever before. They're selling dairy all over the country. And Jace and Mason are thinking of putting a cheese factory in. The local

Amish are willing to work with them in getting it set up, and once it's ready, they said that they'd market it for him in their shops. They seem to think that Double Deuce McBride cheese is going to be huge."

Her mom smiled. Emma knew that her parents loved Mason and what he was doing for the ranch, but she also knew that they thought of her brother often and wondered, like she did, what they had done to make him the way he'd been.

"I want to go and see Dirk's grave too." Emma nodded. "I've had flowers put on it since we've been gone. And I know that Mason has been going to the house. I wanted to...he does a great deal for us that goes beyond being our son-in-law."

"He loves you and Dad very much." Her mom nodded and looked out the window at the men working. "We've talked it over, and Mason and I have...we'd very much like for you to stay with us. One of...Darin wants to buy the house from you and live there. He doesn't have much in the way of money, but Susie and Gerard are lending him enough to put a down payment on it."

"I don't know if I can ever go back there." Emma nodded, knowing how hard it was for her to go by the place, and she'd yet to go inside it. "It needs someone fresh, new. Someone that has nothing to do with what happened there. Perhaps he can bring it to life for us again. I'll talk to your dad. But I think he'll love the idea. Now. Tell me about this Susie. Is she good to Gerard? I've heard good things about her."

"I'm glad you said that." Emma stood up. "I'm having lunch with her and Holly in an hour, and you're going to go as a surprise. Holly is going to have a baby soon, and she's so adorable. Susie is a hoot. And she watches every penny she spends. I just love them both so much."

"Well, of course you do. And she should be watching her pennies. I do, and you know that we don't have to."

Emma nodded as they moved into the main hall to find her dad talking to Mason. They looked good together, the two of them. It looked as if they were plotting. As soon as her dad looked at her, she knew that he'd been told about the baby. And when he picked her up and swung her around the room, she giggled like a child.

"My baby is gonna have a baby. What a wonderful thing to come home to. I'm...I'm so...." Tears filled his eyes and hers too. As he held her, sobbing hard on her shoulder, she held him, looking at Mason as she did. When Dad looked at her, his face wet with tears, she laughed when he wiped them away with his thumb. "I love you, Emma. I can't tell you enough how much I love you and Mason."

"We know, Dad. And we love you very much too." He nodded, still overwhelmed with emotion. "Now. Mom and I are going to have some lunch in town, and you two are going to do some things around here. Remember, no changing things. We have it the way we want it."

~~~

Susie watched the men with the horses. They were loading them onto the trailer like they were gold. She supposed when you paid that much for a horse, they were sort of gold to you. And she really liked the man who was going to train them. He was...well, he was very fatherly toward her and her ponies.

"You got yourself some fine flesh here, missus." She nodded at Sherman when he came to stand beside her. "Them trucks, they're as good as most houses we see around. Got them some air conditioning and all the food and water they want. Every time we stop, somebody will take'em out and air them out while their beds are made. Shoot, we' even put a mint on their pillow for them if'n they're good."

"I was worried how they were going to take the trip. They've only just started being around people." He nodded. She knew that he was a human, but he seemed to know what they all were. "How long will it take you to get back to your ranch?"

"About a week. We want to make sure that they're all right when we get them home. And with this many of them, we want to take our time, get them used to being inside a small place. I doubt any of them have seen much in the way of a barn, much less a trailer. You think?"

"No. They're all wild to some point." She looked over at the stallion that had been the one that Mason had taken her to see. "He's beautiful, isn't he?"

"He is at that. I'm supposed to see if'n you've changed your mind about selling him. I don't think you have, have you?" She shook her head. "We want first pick on his children. I got me a feeling that they're going to be champs. More than champs. I'm thinking that they'll be unstoppable."

She smiled and looked at him. "Maybe I'll put him in a few races and see what he's made of. Could be that I can beat you guys." He looked shocked, and she laughed. "I was just kidding."

"You should do it." She shook her head. "No. You should really do it. My gawd, child. You'll make a fortune off'n him if he only wins one race. His stud services would be…heck fire, we'd pay out the bottom for him coming to sire a few ponies for us. I'm gonna help you too."

"Help me how?" He grinned this time, and she felt like a deer in headlights. "You are very scary right now."

"My son. He's been wanting to branch out on his own. Get out from under his daddy's wing, so to speak. I'm going to talk to him, and he'll come on up here and stay with you while he helps you make a champion. Oh my gawd, this is going to put old Mr. Rose in a pickle." Susie asked if that meant he was going to be mad. "Heck fire no, he's going to love it. And I'm telling you right now, he's gonna work you to death trying to get you to sell him that 'tang of yours once he wins a few. Yes sir, this is going to be a lot of fun."

Emma pulled in the drive just as the last of the horses were being put in the last trailer. The ones that were deemed prize were being brought down to Kentucky by this method, and the rest were being loaded on a train to be taken. The prize horses would arrive later than the others, but they'd be more rested and cared for. Susie was very excited to hear how they worked out.

When an older woman got out of the passenger side of Emma's car, Susie knew who she was immediately. There was no doubt in the world that this was Emma's mother. Susie put out her hand to shake it, but Mrs. McBride pulled her into her arms for a huge hug. Susie felt everything from her, and was glad now that she'd come to see her daughter.

The life and the death of her only son was hurting her. Deep depression was giving her a sadness that the elder woman was having a lot of difficulty in controlling. Not only was she hiding it from her daughter, but from her husband as well, and that, too, was making her ill. If she hadn't come home now, she might not have made it through the next few days. It was that bad for her.

"You're gorgeous! Has Gerard told you that daily?" Susie laughed and looked down at her clothing. "Oh my dear, it's not what you're wearing that makes you lovely, but the freshness of you. You've not a bit of makeup on and you look like a model. And so...my goodness, no wonder you're so happy. You nearly glow with it."

"You must be Mrs. McBride. And I can see now where Emma gets her good looks. You could be her sister." She told her to call her Katie. "All right then. I'm sorry, but I'm running a little behind. The horses are leaving today."

"So I can see." Emma hugged her too as she continued. "What have you decided to name the big boy? Something regal, no doubt."

"Very much so. Palmer pulled a few strings for us, and he actually has a title. And when he gets better at being a good boy, he'll have a pedigree as well." She walked them to the fence, and he came right up to her. Reaching into her pocket, she pulled out an apple and gave it to him. "Ladies, I'd like for you to meet Douglas Mason Gerard McBride. He's named after the man who first found him, the man who saved him, and the ranches that he saved."

"Oh how lovely." Katie reached out to put her hand on his head. But before Susie could caution her to not touch him, that he didn't care for strangers, he pushed his head to her hand and whinnied. "And he's so gentle too."

Emma looked as shocked as Susie felt. Three days ago, Emma had tried to touch him and he'd run to the other side of the corral, not to return until she left the area. Now he was acting like he'd known Katie his entire life. When he moved to Susie again, she put her hand on his head and could feel the understanding from him. He knew — that was all she could think about — he knew that Katie needed comforting.

"Well, we should head out." Susie nodded and asked for ten minutes. As she ran down the hall to shower and change, she thought of the horse. He'd been able to bring her the horses, and she was sure that given time, he'd do it again. She wondered, not for the first time, how he'd known to trust her with this. And how much she and Gerard shared now. Things were, she knew, going to be weirder as she and Gerard figured this out. And they had yet to tell anyone what they could do. For now, she thought it was best if it was just between them.

# Pride of the Double Deuce Series

| Jace | Mason | Gerard |
|:---:|:---:|:---:|
| Pride of the Double Deuce Book 1 | Pride of the Double Deuce Book 2 | Pride of the Double Deuce Book 3 |

## Before You Go...

Share your voice and help guide other readers to these wonderful books. Even if it's only a line or two your reviews help readers discover the author's books so they can continue creating stories that you'll love. Login to your favorite retailer and leave a review. Thank you.

AWARD WINNING, BESTSELLING AUTHOR

Kathi Barton, author of the bestselling series Force of Nature, lives in Nashport, Ohio with her husband Paul. In addition to writing full time Kathi likes to spend time with her eight grandkids, three children and three children-in-laws. She writes to relax and have fun.

Her muse, a cross between Jimmy Stewart and Hugh Jackman brings them to life for her readers in a way that has them coming back time and again for more. Her favorite genre is paranormal romance with a great deal of spice. You can visit Kathi on line and drop her an email if you'd like. She loves hearing from her fans. aaronskiss@gmail.com.

Follow Kathi on her blog:
http://kathisbartonauthor.blogspot.com/